Man Without A Gun

Man Without A Gun

Ray Hogan

DOUBLEDAY & COMPANY, INC.

GARDEN CITY, NEW YORK

1974

B-2

All the characters in this book
are fictitious, and any resemblance to
actual persons, living or dead,
is purely coincidental.

Library of Congress Cataloging in Publication Data

Hogan, Ray, 1908-
    Man without a gun.

    I. Title.
PZ4.H716Man [PS3558.03473] 813'.5'4
ISBN 0-385-06725-9
Library of Congress Catalog Card Number 74-4

For—

GWYNN and SCOTT HENLINE
in Albuquerque

Man Without A Gun

Dow Slater glanced about irritably. A hot, breathless hush filled the bank. It was too quiet, too tense for normalcy. If Pete Reegan and his outlaw bunch showed up at that moment all would know instantly that they had walked into a trap.

The lawman shifted his eyes to the man hunched behind a cabinet on the opposite side of the doorway. Con Williams was a new deputy, on the job for little more than a week. He claimed experience but the tautness of his young features gave Slater cause for worry.

"Why'n the hell don't they come?"

Dow shifted his attention to the head-high partition at the back of the room beyond which Asa Hawkins, the bank's owner, and his clerk, Ollie Davis, were standing. They were endeavoring to maintain a business-as-usual appearance as they peered out from their grill-covered windows, but the shine of sweat was on their faces and both were obviously nervous.

Slater shook his head. "Asa, you sure you don't want me to deputize a couple of men—somebody a little handier with a gun than you and Ollie—and put them back there? Only take a minute or so to—"

"No." Hawkins, a middle-aged man with bushy white

hair and hard black eyes, cut in. "Reegan's been in here before. He sees somebody besides me and Ollie in the cages he's liable to get suspicious and back off—and that I don't want. I aim to make sure he never robs my bank again . . . Don't worry, Marshal, we'll do all right. It's just this waiting around."

The clerk brushed at his face. "I'm starting to think he ain't coming."

"He'll be here," Slater said quietly. "Him and his whole bunch—six, maybe seven just like him. Still a bit early. Word was that they'd wait until the hot part of the day when most folks were inside, out of the heat."

"About that time now," Hawkins murmured. Then: "You sure your information's reliable?"

"It is," the lawman replied and glanced again to Williams. "You all set, Con?"

"All set," the deputy answered.

"Remember this—all of you," Slater continued. "There'll by no shooting unless they start it. We let them get inside the building. Once they're in, the deputy and me will show ourselves. I'll order them to throw down their weapons—"

"Pete Reegan won't give in without a fight," the banker said doubtfully.

"He's a hard one and I'm not underestimating him, but he's smart, too. When he sees there're four guns on him he won't be fool enough to buck the odds. He'll quit."

"But what if he don't?" Ollie Davis muttered.

"He'll find getting back out that door will be the toughest thing he ever tried. That's the reason we've got to hold off, let them all get inside the building before we make our move. Clear?"

"Clear," Hawkins said.

"Yeh, I understand, all right," Davis added, again mopping his face. "It's just that I've never been through something like this before, and to you, I reckon it's old stuff."

Old stuff . . . Dow Slater smiled grimly as he gave the words thought. He was a big man, topping six feet and weighing a solid, muscular two hundred pounds. Dark haired, with gray, almost colorless eyes, a block jaw, and with a full, downcurving mustache, he was one few had ever dared challenge.

He reckoned it was *old stuff* if by that Ollie Davis meant the apprehension of outlaws. A gun marshal, he'd come to Powderville in response to a plea for a lawman who could bring order to a suddenly growing little Kansas town that awoke one day to find itself in the direct path of the railroad.

With several similar jobs under his belt, Slater had applied for the badge. There were a few who opposed the hiring of a man known to be a bit on the ruthless side and perhaps a mite too quick and handy with the big .45 he wore strapped on his leg—why, it was reported that he'd killed at least a dozen men!

The figure was greatly exaggerated but Slater had made no effort to correct it; in his profession he had learned that such magnifications were an asset.

The town council had overruled the objection. After all, it was law and order they sought and it would require a hard-case marshal who was afraid of nobody, who could take on all comers and do whatever was necessary to establish peace and quiet . . . Besides, Dow Slater had a reputation for moving on once he'd accomplished what he'd been hired to do; like as not he'd do just that as soon as Powderville settled down.

Slater had been aware of none of such talk and would have given it no consideration had he been. He was a lawman who enjoyed his work, knew he was good at it and took pride in the fact that outlaws, on the whole, accorded him a healthy respect. Records revealed that once he pinned on a town's nickeled star crime fell off sharply and the lawless gangs that liked to operate in raider fashion found pastures far greener in other localities.

Evidently Pete Reegan and the men who rode with him were unaware that he was now Powderville's marshal, or else figured the ease in which they had cleaned out the town's bank on a previous occasion justified any risk. At any rate they planned to try their hands, and the time, according to a drifter friend of Slater's who had overheard them laying plans, was to be that afternoon.

Although they had never come face to face before Reegan was no stranger to Dow Slater. He knew the outlaw chief as a wily, utterly cool man who so far had never failed in any of his nefarious undertakings which included train robbery, bank and stagecoach holdups, and the plundering of any other business or venture where there was sufficient money to be taken.

Rewards posted for Reegan were numerous and there were those who had attempted to collect them, but always he had outsmarted his would-be captors and escaped, disappearing swiftly, like the fading echo of a gunshot, into the surrounding country.

But this time Pete Reegan was due for a surprise. He would discover the law had planned as carefully as he and there would be no smoothly executed robbery followed by a successful flight into the red clay hills of the Indian Territory or the sheltering Ozarks of Missouri; this time Pete Reegan would fail.

And with him locked behind bars the word would spread quickly along the outlaw trail that Powderville was a town best avoided. But first things first; Reegan was no ordinary outlaw and far from being a greenhorn in his line of endeavor. He was yet to be caught, and to accomplish that there could be no slip-ups.

Slater again let his glance drift about the heat-stuffed room. Deputy Williams, pistol drawn, was staring fixedly at the doorway. Hawkins was idly thumbing a stack of currency in his cage while Ollie Davis, eyes blank, features vacant, was lost in some far-distant field of thought. If there was a weak spot in the net he had cast to ensnare Pete Reegan and his men, it was the bank clerk, Dow concluded, and wished again he'd followed his own inclination and placed more experienced men at the two tellers' windows.

Somewhere along the street a dog began barking. Slater swung his attention to the open doorway. The sound of horses trotting by and the grate of iron-tired wheels slicing through the gritty soil came to him. Powderville was beginning to stir; if Reegan intended to take advantage of the afternoon lull he would have to make his move soon.

"Here comes Turley Woodcock and his missus," Davis said in a tight voice.

Hawkins looked up, a frown on his face. Slater shook his head.

"No call to get jumpy. Do your business with them just the same as if nothing was going on—only do it quick and get them out of here fast as you can."

"Sure, sure, I know," the banker murmured, putting on a fixed smile.

The grating sound had ceased. A man's voice said something at low pitch and a woman laughed quietly. The dog no longer barked but in the trees behind the building a cicada was now filling the hot, still air with its discordant clacking.

Ollie Davis swiped at the glistening sweat on his features once more, mumbling unintelligibly. Hawkins, thin lips drawn into a frozen expression of welcome, stared expectantly at the doorway.

"Slack off, both of you," Slater cautioned.

Darkness filled the entrance to the bank briefly. A tall, wide-shouldered man, browned by hours in the driving sun, dressed in coarse but clean farm clothing, stepped inside. A woman, somewhat younger and pretty in a healthy, well-rounded way, moved in beside him.

"Howdy, Mr. Hawkins," Woodcock greeted, raising his hand. "Dropping by to pay—"

His words broke off suddenly. He rocked to one side

as four men, their faces covered by neckerchief masks, pushed roughly by him and his wife.

A fifth man, tall, wearing an ankle-length brown duster, a flat crowned plainsman's hat with a fancy brass studded, horsehair band, remained in the doorway. Masked also, and with the hat tipped well forward, only his eyes, glittering like small, polished shoe buttons, were visible in his lean face. He held a pistol in each hand.

"Nobody move!" he barked in a harsh voice.

2

The woman cried out as she went to her knees. Woodcock, struggling to keep his balance, whirled angrily. Slater cursed silently. Reegan had played it smart. He had held off until there were others in the bank thus guaranteeing no resistance.

"Hold your fire!" Slater shouted.

At the same time Ollie Davis opened up with his weapon. His first bullet caught the outlaw directly in front of him in the chest, driving him backward into Woodcock.

More guns began to blast and the room abruptly was a turmoil of deafening sound, swirling smoke, and a woman's piercing screams. Slater, whipping out his pistol, dropped the outlaw firing at Davis, and then spun to face Reegan.

The man, never entirely inside the bank, stood spread-legged in the doorway, triggering both his weapons blindly into the blue-black haze. Rage soared within Dow at sight of such cold-blooded callousness. He snapped a shot at the outlaw leader, cursing himself for his haste when the bullet missed, splintering wood near Pete Reegan's head.

In the next moment Mrs. Woodcock broke through the

pall and staggered toward him. Her face was a distorted mask of horror and pain as she clutched at her breast.

"Oh, my God—who'll look after my babies?" she shrilled, and collapsed at his feet.

Grim, Slater stepped over her and rushed for the doorway. Reegan and one of his men were hurrying into the open. Vaguely, from the tail of an eye, he noted the bodies sprawled on the floor—Woodcock, Con Williams, the outlaws, the two shapes slumped behind the grilled windows in the partition, and, of course, the woman.

He reached the entrance and stepped into the street, ignoring the shouts of the crowd that was beginning to gather. Pete Reegan and his one remaining follower were hurrying shapes ducking around the corner of the building. Gun in hand, the lawman raced after them. He reached the end of the structure. Reegan had already rounded the back, but the man with him was still in sight. He twisted half about in stride, raised his pistol. Slater drove a bullet into his heart before he could press the trigger of his weapon.

Slater continued on, gained the back of the building, swore. Reegan had disappeared behind a row of sagging sheds and outbuildings that stood along the alley.

Thumbing cartridges from his belt and reloading as he ran, Dow proceeded more cautiously. The outlaw could be waiting behind any one of the small buildings, holding off for just the moment when he would be afforded a clear and easy shot.

Slater reached the first of the sheds, halted and peered around the corner of the weathered structure. The weedy alley was empty. Taut, the lawman dropped back to the front of the old buildings, and trotted to the far end of the row. The outlaws would have picketed their horses somewhere close by; along the sheds was the logical place.

But there was no sign of the animals, or of Pete Reegan. Slater frowned, puzzling over the problem. Back in the street he could hear shouting coming from in front of the bank; most of the townspeople, roused from their afternoon lethargy by the gunshots, were now on hand. And then in that moment he heard the sudden hammer of a horse as it pounded off from somewhere in the trees to his right.

Reegan . . . The outlaw had gotten to his mount, stationed farther away from the buildings than could be expected, and was making good his escape. Dow broke into a hard run, gained the last of the sheds. Several hundred yards down a narrow lane to his right a boil of dust hung in the still air. Pete Reegan had gotten away again.

For a long breath Slater stood in silence and watched. Finally wheeling, he started back to the bank. A heavy soberness filled him and a quick vision of Mrs. Woodcock staggering toward him, her face torn with pain and fear, kept passing before his eyes. It had been as if she was accusing him.

Moving past the lifeless outlaw sprawled in the dust, he rounded the corner of the building. Two dozen or more persons were gathered in the street before its entrance. They gave way, formed a path for him as he stalked silently through their midst.

Inside the bank he drew to a slow halt. Smoke still drifted lazily about and the smell of burnt gunpowder was strong. Three or four men stood in the center of the room staring numbly about at the bodies littering the floor. There was no sound other than the shuffling noise outside the door of those craning to get a better view.

"God in heaven!" someone said in an awed voice. "They're all dead—all of them."

Slater did not stir. Horror and revulsion was building within him as he looked about. The voice had been right; not one of them—Hawkins, Deputy Williams, Ollie Davis, the Woodcocks—had lived through the raid. And dead with them were three of the outlaws while a fourth lay outside. Only Pete Reegan and he had survived.

Unaccountably chilled, Dow Slater drew himself up stiffly, a man suddenly and irrevocably stricken by the senseless slaughter in which he had participated.

"What—what happened?" a voice asked at his shoulder.

The lawman turned slowly. Never before had he felt as he did—a heaviness, a glowing sort of hatred for and rejection of what he had always heretofore considered duty.

"Was a try at robbing the bank," he murmured.

"But all these folks—"

Slater shook his head wearily, stepping back as a man, a black leather bag clamped under one arm, bustled past. It was Doc Ivor, the town's physician as well as coroner, and a member of the council. The medical man paused, eyes spreading slightly as he took in the scene, and then knelt over the woman.

"Ain't no use, Doc," one of the men said. "None of them's alive."

Slater, looking on woodenly, felt a hand grip his arm. It was Henry Eamons, the mayor.

"How could something like this happen, Marshal? Was my understanding you had it all planned out."

"I did," Slater answered in a falling voice. "Just that it all went wrong."

He could have explained that Ollie Davis had lost his head and had begun the shooting that set off the massacre, but it would serve no purpose other than to blacken the name of a man now dead.

"There's another body laying outside," someone volunteered from the doorway.

Eamons asked quickly: "Reegan?"

"No. He got away."

The mayor fell silent, head wagging slowly from side to side as if still unable to believe what his eyes beheld.

"The Woodcocks—how'd they—"

"Reegan and his bunch laid back, waited 'til somebody came to the bank," Slater said in a dull voice. "Happened to be them. Outlaws figured to use them as a sort of shield, and maybe later as hostages if they needed them."

"Hell of a thing, killing a woman. Why would they want to shoot her?"

Again the remembrance of Mrs. Woodcock staggering toward him floated through Dow Slater's mind, once more her anguished cries echoed in his ears. The bitterness within him intensified.

"Can't answer that. Likely was a stray bullet."

"Stray bullet kills you just as dead as one that's pointed at you," a bystander observed unnecessarily.

The bank was fairly well crowded now, many of the onlookers in the street having worked their way inside. Doc Ivor had straightened out the bodies, laying them in a neat row, and had sent for blankets to cover them until they could be moved. He had also dispatched someone to look after the Woodcock children until arrangements could be made for their care.

"You getting up a posse and going after Reegan?" Eamons asked.

Slater digested the question slowly as the void within him deepened steadily. His bleak gaze traveled over the dead faces, the slack figures lined up side by side awaiting the undertaker—and the graveyard. He shook his head.

"No," he replied in a low, tight way, "I'm through."

"Through?" Eamons echoed, surprised. "What the hell's that mean? You sure don't aim to let him get away—go scot-free do you?"

"Get somebody else," Dow said, taking his star from a pocket and handing it to the mayor.

"You mean you're quitting?"

Slater nodded. Unbuckling the heavy belt encircling his waist, he tossed it and the bone-handled .45 that had been his constant companion for so many years, into a corner of the room.

"Quitting you, quitting the law," he said, starting for the door. "If I ever take up a gun again I hope God strikes me dead before I can use it!"

3

The room was in utter silence. Ivor, standing at the end of the partition, studied Slater thoughtfully. Outside the cicada had resumed its shrill racket and the odor of gunpowder still hung in the cloudy air.

"You mean that?" Henry Eamons asked incredulously, finally breaking the hush.

Dow had halted at the door. "I'm done with killing."

"But they were outlaws—leastwise some of them were."

"Killing's killing, no matter who," Slater said heavily.

Eamons shrugged. "Can't understand you, Marshal. You've been through this before—worse, more than likely. What makes this one different? Sure, it's a bad thing and real unfortunate that the Woodcocks got caught in the middle and that Asa and Ollie stopped bullets, but that's how things go sometimes."

Slater, his hard-cornered face still, his eyes remote, made no comment. Doc Ivor sighed gustily.

"Let it be, Henry," he said softly.

"No need for you to feel the way you do," the mayor said, ignoring the medical man. "Go on over to the Palace, have a couple of drinks. That'll make you see things different. Or maybe it'll be better if you'll get yourself good and drunk—"

"Shut up, Henry," Ivor broke in, his voice sharp.

"When you sober up, you'll find your gun and badge in your office," Eamons continued. "Can decide then what to do about Pete Reegan."

Dow Slater said nothing. Turning, he faced the man, a small, bitter smile on his lips, nodded, and then stepped out into the fading sunlight. A half hour later he rode off into the south, taking the trail for Dodge City.

He traveled slowly, indifferently, passing through small settlements, encountering other pilgrims, and ignoring all as if they did not exist. He halted only when it was necessary to rest his sorrel horse or when personal hunger and fatigue forced him to do so. He was as a man in a depthless trance, neither caring nor not caring, seeing and yet blind. It took him a week to reach Dodge City, a trip ordinarily requiring three days at most.

There he stabled the gelding, sought out a small saloon below the Deadline where there would be no possibility of meeting an old acquaintance, and in the company of a blowzy redheaded woman who gravitated to his table immediately upon arrival, Dow proceeded to get himself roaring drunk.

Five days later, poorer by fifty dollars or so, and stone-cold sober, he mounted the sorrel and left Dodge, heading due west this time. He felt better, somehow relieved and more at peace with himself, but his determination to not again carry a gun was unaltered.

Oddly, for a man who had more or less lived by such for most of his life, he gave little thought to the change that had overtaken him. It had happened, had quickly become a part of his nature as permanent as if it had always existed.

He recognized the fact he was a man finished with using a gun, and that was it. No other explanation was necessary. He'd find a different way of life, another means by which to support himself, and with that consoling thought in mind the bitter self-recrimination that had flayed him began to fade gradually.

He had ridden out of Powderville with only the clothing he wore, leaving all else accumulated in a lifetime behind. There'd been three double eagles and some change in his pockets and that now had been reduced to a little less than a third of the original amount; locating work was a prospect for the near future, he realized.

Getting hired on as a lawman somewhere would be simple if he so desired. A half a hundred towns would welcome him and his experience once he had made known his identity and detailed his references. But such could not be farther from his mind; pinning on a star went hand in hand with wearing and using a gun—and that was out.

A job as a cowpuncher, a stagecoach driver, even a barkeep, if all else failed, was what he'd settle for. There had to be other ways he could make a living besides carrying a weapon.

He wondered about Pete Reegan one day as he drifted indifferently along the well-beaten trail to Santa Fe. Had someone gone in pursuit of the outlaw, brought him in to face justice as he'd hoped to do?

It wasn't likely. There'd been no one left in Powderville capable of undertaking such a task. Con Williams, his deputy, was dead and it would have taken time to call in a lawman from the outside to take charge. It was possible Henry Eamons had hastily assembled a posse to give chase, but their efforts would have gone for naught. Pete Reegan was an old hand at eluding pursuit especially when it was by a party of amateurs.

Reegan would still be free, probably holed up somewhere, and while he had failed in his efforts to fatten his purse with gold from the Powderville bank, he was little worse off. The loss of the men who had accompanied him would mean nothing; he had only to pass the word and he'd have a dozen replacements clamoring to line up with him. Pete was known to be expert in his field and those fortunate enough to partner with him could expect to fare well.

But it had been a close call for the outlaw and it could be he would elect to move on, find new fields where he was still unknown. One thing sure, he would not soon forget those brief, violent moments in the Powderville bank when he'd seen his men go down and death had been but a breath away from him, nor would he forget the lawman who had brought it all about.

Slater had given that considerable thought as the days wore on and the miles of his back trail piled up steadily. If ever he came face to face with the outlaw he could expect the man to seek his vengeance, and without a weapon how could he defend himself?

He didn't know, and in his new state of mind, didn't

actually care. He'd manage, somehow, if and when the moment came—if ever it did. Until then he'd waste no time anticipating it.

He reached the old Spanish capital in New Mexico Territory, tarried briefly and rode on, crossing the broad flat west to where it broke off into a wide green valley lush with trees, grass, and bright blossomed flowers.

Reaching the river called the Rio Grande, he followed its meandering course southward, past several slumbering Indian pueblos and small villages, skirting a row of long dead volcanoes which were dwarfed by towering mountains lying across the valley to the east.

At a small settlement called Socorro he swung west, having no desire to face a burning, waterless desert that he was told had been named by early explorers, the *Jornada del Muerto* (Journey of the Dead), riding instead into high, pine covered hills that offered peace and quiet.

And then days later, weeks after those flaming moments in Powderville, and still at loose ends, he found himself entering a broad valley that unfurled before him like a vast green carpet. A fairly new sign, in the shape of an arrow and pointing indefinitely into the area, bore the words: SHIBOLEM 3 MILES.

Shibolem . . . It was a strange name for a town and it brought a stir of interest . . . He needed a job. He'd look for one here.

4

He pushed on, following out a single-track road that wound downward between scrub cedar and piñon trees, clumps of oak brush and other stringy growth until he broke out onto a wide grassy flat. It was near sundown and the last golden rays of light were spreading a soft, amber haze across the country and pointing up the vivid colors of wild marigold and purple verbena that dotted the gentle slopes and shallow swales.

The valley broadened as he moved deeper into its lush depth. He could see the dim, smoky outlines of high mountains both to the east and west, reckoned they could be at least fifty miles apart. Far ahead the land seemed to rise and flow onto a plain. Mexico would lie somewhere in that direction.

Shortly buildings appeared on the horizon, all hunched closely together as if to ward off by their mutual presence the vast loneliness of the surrounding, empty world. As he drew nearer he saw that they were placed in a pocket of meadow created by a bend in a river, that most were the usual one-story, false-fronted structures common throughout the frontier.

SHIBOLEM . . . He encountered a second sign at the beginning of the one street along which the structures stood in a short, double row facing one another. Residences were visible in the areas beyond the business district. In the soft light of day's end the town appeared tranquil, friendly, and the stir of interest within Dow Slater heightened, crystallized. Here was where he would stop.

Spurring the weary sorrel lightly, he continued on down the dusty roadway. A half a dozen or so persons were moving along the board sidewalks. Three men lounged on the porch of the Happy Jack Saloon, and above on the gallery a woman in a red and blue dress, her face heavily rouged and powdered, eyed him speculatively.

Tilton's General Store . . . The Home Cafe . . . Hurd's Livery Stable . . . The Calico Girl Drinking, Gambling & Dancing . . . Mason's Saddlery & Gun Shop . . . Joe Johnson Feed & Seed Co . . . Turner's Ladies & Gents Clothing. Also Childrens . . . The Prairie Rose Hotel . . . Deputy Sheriff & Jail . . . A few other establishments. Idly, Slater read the names, ran them through his mind, registering each.

Coming to the end of the street, aware now of the curious attention being accorded him as a stranger by the loafers at the Happy Jack as well as from others along the way, he swung the gelding into the hitchrack in front of the livery stable and halted. For a time he remained motionless on the saddle, a big, square-shouldered shape in the dusk, and then dismounted.

Moving deliberately, he wrapped the leathers around the tie bar and crossed to the stable's entrance. An elderly man came out of the shadows, wiping his hands on a rag and nodded slightly.

"Can I help you?"

Dow jerked his thumb at the sorrel. "Horse of mine's about done in. Like to put him up for the night."

"What I'm in business for. Be fifty cents."

Slater dug into his pocket for the necessary coin, handed it to the stableman. "There be any objections to me sleeping in the loft?"

The hostler frowned, shrugged. "All right with me long as you don't do no smoking . . . You be riding out in the morning?"

Slater glanced back up the street. "No. Fact is I'm looking for a job. You Hurd?"

The man bobbed. "That's me—but there ain't no work here. Hardly enough to keep me busy." He paused, considered Dow closely. "You flat busted?"

"Just about."

"Well, you do some asking around you might find something. What can you do?"

"Nothing in particular. Take most anything."

"Ought to make it easy," Hurd said drily, moving toward the hitchrack. "You can sort of headquarter out of my place if you like 'til you get lined up. Still be four bits a night for the sorrel, howsomever."

"Suits me fine," Slater said, watching the man unwind the gelding's reins and head toward the wide entrance to the livery barn.

Following them into the bulking, shadow-filled structure, Dow helped the stable owner strip his gear and then waited while the sorrel was moved into a stall and a quantity of hay and grain put in the manger.

"I'll rub him down myself—later," he said as Hurd stepped back into the runway.

"Help yourself. Plenty of gunny sacks over there in the corner."

"There a place around here where I can wash up a bit?"

Hurd waved vaguely toward the rear of the barn. "Trough back there," he said and glanced toward the entrance to the barn. Two women, one young with a red scarf around her head, the other much older, in a light buggy were swinging into the wagonyard adjoining the stable. The stableman muttered something under his breath relative to non-paying customers and tramped off to his quarters at the end of the runway.

Walking to the rear of the building, Slater located the water trough, and stripping to the waist, washed himself. Drying off as best he could with a small rag he found hanging on a nail, he returned to the street. It had been weeks, it seemed, since he'd had a good meal. Food had held little appeal for him since leaving Powderville and he had eaten what he could get when he could get it and then only because of necessity. Now, however, his appetite had returned and was in full clamor.

Standing in the entrance to the stable, he glanced along the street. A short distance down the way he located the Home Cafe. A tall, dark-haired woman wearing a white apron over her dress was lighting the bracket lamps at each end of the large window. The yellow glow was touching her features giving them a soft, blurred look. She turned away and at once he moved out into the street.

A cool breeze was drifting through the town as he angled through the inches-deep dust, and again he was conscious of the attention accorded him by passers-by. At first he had assumed such was because he was a stranger in their midst, and then it came to him that the fact he was unarmed was creating the interest. He had never paid much attention to it before but looking about it did seem that every man who walked wore a gun, likely would feel only half dressed without a weapon. Such would have been the case with him a few weeks ago. Weeks? It seemed months—years, even—since he left Powderville!

Stepping up onto the walk he halted at the cafe's screen door. Inside the place appeared spotlessly clean with white cloths on the half dozen or so tables, dust-free painted floor and unmarked floral design paper on the walls. He could see two patrons, the girl with the red scarf and the elderly woman who undoubtedly was her mother since the resemblance was apparent.

Slater hesitated. This was no place for him—not with him needing a shave and haircut as badly as he did and with his clothes in the shape they were. Best he settle for one of the saloons where . . .

"We're open. Come in."

He glanced up at the invitation. It was the tall woman he'd seen placing the lamps in the window. She was standing in the doorway, holding the screen open for him to enter. There was a smile on her lips and he saw she was even more attractive up close than from a distance.

He shook his head. "Just came in off the trail. Not exactly spruced up for a fine place like this."

Her smile widened. "You look all right to me, Mr.—"

"Slater. Dow Slater."

"Mr. Slater. I'm Judith Hazelwood. This is my restaurant and I assure you you're welcome."

Dow nodded, and pulling off his hat, stepped up into the room, and for the first time since those moments of violence in the Powderville bank he felt completely at ease with himself and the world.

5

The woman had pulled back, and crossing to a corner table, Slater sat down. The air was saturated with the cheery odor of cooking food and for a time he remained motionless absorbing the inviting smells and enjoying the pleasant surroundings as a man too long deprived of the ordinary good things in life would do.

And then he caught himself, glanced around. The girl and her mother were watching him. A faint smile of amusement was on the younger woman's lips. Dow nodded automatically, only casually noting her fairness, and turned his attention to Judith Hazelwood approaching him from the kitchen which apparently lay beyond a door in the back wall. She carried a cup and saucer in one hand, a small pot of coffee in the other.

Placing the cup before him she filled it and set the white granite container close by for his convenience. Folding her arms, she looked at him questioningly. Judith was in her late twenties, he supposed, had deep blue eyes to go with her dark hair.

"What can I get you, Mr. Slater?"

"Steak and potatoes will do fine—"

"Along with hot biscuits and gravy and some baked green chili on the side?"

"Sounds just right," he said and watched her turn, move off toward the kitchen and disappear through the doorway.

Almost at once a young Mexican girl in her early teens entered bringing silverware, a red and white checked cloth napkin and a glass of water. She set them before him in silence, hurried to where the two women were sitting and began to pick up their dirty dishes.

Slater shifted his attention to the street, easily visible through the clean glass of the window. A good many shoppers were abroad now, strolling about in the light of several post lamps as well as those glowing in the stores. Shibolem was a cattle town he guessed, judging from the number of men dressed in range clothing. Coming into the settlement he hadn't really thought about it, but now reviewing the country in his mind he could see that it would be ideal for raising beef.

The screen door jerked open, banged noisily against its frame. Two men came in, one staggering uncertainly. Both were wearing guns and as Judith, hearing them arrive, appeared, they halted in the center of the room.

"We've come for supper," the drunk one said, bracing himself with a hand on the back of a chair.

The woman shook her head. "Not here. Place you want's down the street—the Calico Girl."

The puncher's jaw jutted belligerently. "We're aiming to eat here," he said thickly. "This here's a cafe, ain't it?"

The drunk's partner laid a hand on his shoulder. "Come on, Tip, let's go. We can't get no liquor here anyway."

"The hell we can't!" the puncher shouted, pointing at the young girl. "That there little Mex'll fetch us a bottle."

The girl dodged his groping hand, scurried off into the kitchen. Judith Hazelwood, lips set, stepped up to the pair.

"Get out," she ordered quietly.

The women at the back table were watching in strained silence. Abruptly the younger one rose to her feet.

"You heard Judith, Tip! Get out or I'll call Ed Gault."

The drunk swayed about, faced her, a slack-lipped grin on his face. "Now, just what'll he do? That there deputy badge he's wearing don't mean nothing to me! Nope, we're setting us down and having us some grub right here, and that little Mex is going to get us a bottle or I aim to take this here place apart!"

Slater pushed back from his table, drew himself upright. In two long strides he reached the drunk. Catching him by the collar of his coarse shirt, he jerked him about, shoved him toward the door.

"You heard the lady—get out."

Tip stumbled, righted himself, wheeled. "Who you think you're pushing?

"Don't see as it matters who," Slater replied indifferently, glancing at the drunk's friend. "Look after him."

"I don't need no looking after!" Tip shouted and reached for the pistol on his hip.

Slater's arm shot out. His big hand clamped down upon that of the puncher, powerful fingers crushing it against the metal weapon. Tip yelled in pain, tried to jerk away.

Slater caught the man by the neck with his free hand, spun him about. Booting open the screen door, he threw the man into the street.

Stepping back, he held the screen for the second puncher to move by. There was a hard twist to his lips when he spoke.

"Saying it again, you'd best look out for your drunk friend. Could get himself hurt."

The man mumbled something, crossed to where Tip was picking himself up slowly. A half a dozen passers-by had paused, were looking on smilingly. Others farther down the way were hurrying up to see what it was all about. Slater remained framed in the doorway until the pair had moved on, and then wheeling resumed his place at his table.

Judith halted before him. "Want to thank you. I don't often get their kind in here."

"Always plenty of them around, seems," he replied.

The incident had failed to even disturb his normal breathing, she noticed, studying him quietly. Then: "You're a lawman, aren't you?"

"Was—once. Not any more."

"I thought so—just from the way you handled Tip." She broke off abruptly, whirled, started for the kitchen. "Your steak—I hope it's not overcooked!"

The door swung open again. A dark, husky young man wearing a star burst in. He glanced about, stepped quickly to the table where the girl and her mother sat.

"There some trouble here, Glenna?" he asked, swinging his attention back to Slater.

"All over," the girl answered. "Tip Weber and that Ben Denver came in. They were both drunk, tried to start something with Judith. That gentleman over there," she added, nodding at Dow, "threw them out."

The deputy wheeled, crossed the room to Slater. His broad face was angry. "Obliged to you, mister, but next time you call me. I'm the law around here."

Dow Slater shrugged, took a swallow of his coffee. Ed Gault, the girl had named him. His star bore the black lettered inscription, DEPUTY SHERIFF.

"Not aiming to cut in on you, Deputy. Just wasn't time."

Judith emerged from the kitchen, a platter heaped with food in one hand, a plate of biscuits in the other. She smiled at Gault, centered the meal before Slater, an apologetic look in her eyes.

"I hope the meat isn't too done—"

"Be fine," Slater said, taking up his knife and fork.

Gault watched him briefly, spun on a heel and returned to where Glenna and her mother sat. "Can use a cup of coffee—and a piece of pie," he called over his shoulder as he settled down.

Judith glanced toward the kitchen. "Teresa, bring some of that peach pie and a cup of coffee for Deputy Gault," then brought her attention back to Dow. "Are you just riding through?"

He gave that consideration as he chewed on a piece of the meat. It was tender and to his liking, although, as she had feared, a bit well-cooked to suit him exactly.

"Depends. Been just sort of drifting. Kind of like the looks of things around here, however."

"It's a nice little town," Judith said, taking up the granite pot and refilling his cup. "Where are you from?"

"Kansas."

She did not pursue the question further, sensing in his reply a reluctance to be more specific. "I hope you don't have any trouble with Tip Weber."

"Don't worry about it . . . Want to say this is the best meal I've ever had. You're a mighty fine cook, if it's you that done the cooking."

He was surprised at the ease that had overtaken him. It was like the old days, the time long before Powderville and the other towns, when he was first learning his trade and a gun had not yet become second nature to him.

"I do all of the cooking," Judith said. "Teresa helps with the dishes and the cleaning."

"Thought maybe your husband ran the kitchen."

"I'm a widow. My husband was killed in the war."

"Right sorry to hear that."

Somewhere out in the night a gunshot flatted through the hush. Ed Gault arose immediately, went to the door and stepped out onto the walk. He glanced about and then started at a fast pace for some point down the way.

"Gault keep things pretty straight around here?" Dow wondered, finishing off the last of the steak and potatoes.

"Oh, yes, but we don't have many problems. The sheriff's up at the county seat, and if something comes along the deputy can't handle, he sends for him . . . Are you interested in getting a lawman's job?"

"No." Slater's reply was quick, flat. "Just asking . . . Am looking for work, however."

"What sort? If you were a lawman once—"

"I'm not interested in becoming one again."

"I see," Judith murmured, once more filling his cup. "About all there is in these parts is ranching. You might ask around—"

"I'm looking for a hand," the girl, Glenna, said from across the room. "And I think you're just the kind to do the job."

Judith's lips tightened and a frown of annoyance flickered across her face. Slater looked beyond her to the girl.

"That so?"

Glenna rose, moved toward Slater. He started to get to his feet. She waved him back, said, "Keep your seat. I'm not used to politeness," and smiled at Judith. "You don't mind if I talk a little business, do you?"

The cafe woman shrugged. "Of course not . . . I'll get more coffee," and collecting the dishes from Dow's table, turned for the kitchen.

Glenna was small, pert, had honey-blond hair, brown eyes and a quick, wide smile. She was dressed in a white shirtwaist and gray corduroy riding skirt below which black, high-heeled boots could be seen. Slipping into a chair opposite Slater, she extended a hand across the table.

"I'm Glenna Darrow—and that's my mother. We own the Circle D ranch. You know anything about cattle?"

"Some—not much," Dow replied, and stated his name.

"I know," the girl said. "Heard you give it to Judith. You want a job working on my ranch?"

Dow studied her quietly. She was a direct, straight-to-the-point sort of person, undoubtedly had a will of her own.

"Like I said, don't know much about raising cattle—"

"Not necessary. That's my end of it and besides, I've got hired help that don't savvy anything else. What I want is a man who can handle himself and other men."

"What makes you think I can fill the bill?" Slater asked, faintly amused by the girl's manner.

"Way you took care of Tip Weber for one thing—"

"Just a drunk. Anybody could've done that."

"If they'd wanted—and dared. Tip's a hard case. Expect you saw that but it didn't stop you from doing what was necessary . . . You interested?"

Judith reappeared with fresh coffee and a cup for her own use. Sitting down at the table she filled Slater's empty container and her own, then settled back. Glenna Darrow flicked her with a sly glance, looked again to Dow.

"Well?"

"Not sure I can come up to what you're looking for. What'll the job be, exactly?"

"Well, it stacks up this way. We don't have a big ranch and I've been running it since Pa died. Been no easy chore—can tell you that. Place never has paid off like it should, even when Pa was alive. Just couldn't seem to get things together somehow."

"Trouble with other ranchers?"

"No, not that. They don't bother us—don't help us any, either. Just sort of let matters take their course. I expect they all feel we'll go under someday."

"What's the problem, then?"

Glenna frowned, puckered her mouth and started to speak. She hesitated as the door opened to admit a man and woman who nodded genially to everyone present. Judith, her features prim, got to her feet, conducted the pair to a table at the back of the room.

"It's the hired hands more'n anything," Glenna continued, glancing over her shoulder at Mrs. Darrow. The older woman was staring absently through the window. "They've been with us for years—ever since Pa started the Circle D, in fact. Mother won't let me get rid of them —even if I could."

Slater shrugged. "No reason if they know their job."

"There's plenty of reason!" Glenna flared, and then in a lower voice added, "They just can't do the work any more. I know that keeping them on is the main reason the ranch has gone downhill for the past few years—and why we're in the pickle we're in."

Dow sipped his coffee, waited for her to explain further. Judith had gone into the kitchen and the Mexican girl was bringing in silverware and other necessary items for the new customers.

"I haven't told this to Mother yet, but we're on our last legs. If we don't come up with some money this summer from selling part of the herd, we're finished."

"Sounds simple enough."

"It's not. Cowhands we've got aren't capable of making the drive—even the short one I'm planning. You can."

"Never been on a cattle drive in my life."

"No worry there. They can look after the herd, your job will be to get it through."

"Where's the railhead?"

"Place called McCoy. About ten days' drive from here —but we can go into that later if you hire on."

Dow Slater turned his attention to the street. It was full dark now and there were fewer people about than earlier . . . Shibolem would be a good place to call a halt, start a new life—one wherein a gun would play no part. But Glenna Darrow should know that.

"Willing to pay a little extra," Glenna went on. "Fifty a month and keep. Regular hands draw thirty but I figure you'll be worth more."

"Maybe not—"

The girl frowned. "What makes you say that?"

Slater slapped his leg. "I don't carry a gun."

She frowned. "Noticed that, just figured you'd left yours on the peg. You got some special reason why you won't wear one?"

"Yeh—personal."

Glenna eyed him thoughtfully. Then: "Up to you, of course, but I think you'll change your mind and start packing one sooner or later. Only thing I'm interested in is getting my cows to McCoy and collecting the money so's I can put the ranch on a paying basis. I figure you're the one who can help me do it. If you can manage it without a gun, it's jake with me . . . You want the job or not?"

Dow grinned at her bluntness, nodded. "I want it—long as you know where I stand."

Glenna gave him her quick smile. "Good—it's settled. Expect if there's anybody that can live in this country without a six-gun, it's you . . . Now, you want to ride out with us tonight or you waiting until tomorrow?"

"As soon wait for morning."

Slater didn't know why. It didn't matter and refusing Glenna meant he'd be spending the night in Hurd's hayloft instead of in a bunkhouse, but Judith Hazelwood was pleasant company and he enjoyed being with her.

"Suit yourself," Glenna said, rising. "We'll look for you in the morning. Ask anybody—they'll be able to tell you where the Circle D is."

Wheeling, the girl returned to her mother who got slowly to her feet, and then together they moved toward the door. Abruptly Glenna paused, glanced back.

"Judith—put the suppers on our tab," she called. "Slater's, too. Good night."

6

Dow glanced around. Judith stood framed in the kitchen's
door, her eyes following the Darrow women as they
moved off into the street. Her features were expression-
less, but as she turned toward Slater, a wedge of hot pie
on a saucer in her hands, her lips parted into a smile.

"Glenna's quite a girl," she murmured, setting the
dessert in front of him.

He nodded, reached into his pocket and withdrew several coins, laid them on the table. "I'll pay for my meal,"
he said, picking up his fork and attacking the pie.

Judith's smile widened. "I thought you would," she
said, drawing a half a dollar from the loose change. "This
will cover it . . . I guess you took the job."

"Not yet. Riding out and hashing it over with them in
the morning."

The woman shrugged. "You could do better."

It was impossible to miss the disapproval in her manner. "Anything wrong with working for the Darrow
outfit?"

"Haven't said there was—and it certainly is none of my
business. You can do as you please, only there's not much
point to it. Lining up with one of the other ranchers
would make more sense."

He looked at her questioningly. "Still haven't laid out any reasons."

"Well, like as not there won't be any Darrow ranch by Christmas. It's been going down ever since John Darrow died—wasn't much even before that. And now with Glenna trying to run it, it's even less."

"She did say they were in trouble, needed money. Figures to cure that by selling off some stock. My job'd be to get the herd to the railhead. Says she can't depend on the cowhands she has to do it."

"That'll be true. There are only four of them and they're all too old to be working . . . She tell you about her brother, Royce?"

"Brother? No, didn't mention him."

"You'll be saddled with him, too. He's younger than Glenna—a drunk and a plain no-account. Add him to the four old men you'll have to look after—along with the herd. The Circle D's broke, owes everybody including me. They haven't paid wages in months."

Slater gave that thought. It explained why Glenna Darrow was unable to hire on a new and younger crew, a suggestion he'd started to make to her. There simply was no money and she was gambling everything on the stock he would be driving to the railhead at McCoy.

"Something else you ought to know—Glenna's engaged to marry Ed Gault."

"Figured there was something between them."

"They'd do it tonight if Ed had his way but she won't agree to it until she's got the ranch on a paying basis. Claims she owes that much to her family."

"What if she fails?"

Judith's shoulders stirred. "I think that's what Ed Gault's really hoping for. That would settle the question quick and he could go ahead with his plans."

Slater paused, rubbed at his whiskered jaw. "If he's so set on marrying her, why don't he forget that badge he's wearing and go in with her on running the ranch? Seems to me that'd be the answer for both of them."

"First place Glenna won't hear of it—she's set on doing it on her own. And in the second place Ed's not willing to give up being a lawman. The sheriff's an old man and plans to give up the job next year when election comes around. Ed Gault's in line to take his place. No doubt he likes that idea more than playing second fiddle to Glenna's being a rancher."

Dow grinned. "Beginning to get the idea you're not exactly crazy about her."

Judith bristled. "That's neither here nor there! I just don't care for the way she acts—so high and mighty and all that—"

"Putting on a big front with the seat of her britches out," Slater offered.

Judith stared at him for a long moment and then laughed. "That's it exactly . . . But it's the Darrows' business, not mine."

"Yeh, reckon it is," he said gently. "Obliged to you for the information, however. Sort of sets me straight on what to expect."

"Only fair that you know." She reached for the coffee-pot, abandoned it when he shook his head. "I can't picture you as a cowhand."

"I'm not. Wore a star most of my life."

She nodded approvingly. "Fits you better," she said, getting up. "I—I hope you'll drop by once in a while, take a meal with me. The Darrow ranch isn't far from town."

Slater, on his feet, picked up his change and dropping it into a pocket stepped out from behind the table. Across the room the elderly couple were dawdling over their coffee and pie. Both watched him with interest.

"I'll be back," Dow said. "Can bank on that."

He started toward the door, paused as Judith reached out and caught him by the arm.

"Be careful. Tip Weber won't—"

Slater shrugged, smiled. "Forget it. His kind's a dime a dozen. I'm not worried."

"Maybe you should be—you're not even wearing a gun!"

"That's part of the past," he said, pushing open the door. "Good night."

Judith stood for a few moments watching his high-shouldered outline fade into the darkness of the street, and then turning, began to collect the dishes from the table. The voice of Mr. Caruthers, sitting with his wife, reached her.

"Don't recollect seeing that big fellow around here before."

"He's a stranger," she replied. "Going to work for the Darrows."

"We heard what he done to Tip Weber. Wish't I'd a seen him doing it."

Judith smiled, moved on into the kitchen. She set the dishes in the washpan, and, as Teresa hurried up with a kettle of boiling water, came back about and retraced her steps to the front. The Carutherses were leaving, and the usual neat stack of coins was beside one of the plates. They ordered the same thing every night, never varying, and thus always knew exactly how much cash would be required for their check.

"Thank you, folks," she called after them.

Caruthers, ushering his wife out onto the walk, bobbed and smiled. "You're welcome . . . Good night."

Judith murmured her response, and following them to the door, dropped the screen's hook into its eye, closed the solid panel and locked it. Stepping then to the window she turned down the lamps and blew out the flame, plunging the room into shadows. There were still a few lights aglow in the street, and sinking into a chair, she sighed heavily.

It had been a busy day with many of the ranchers bringing their families in for weekend shopping, and as was the custom, taking the noon meal at her restaurant. Now, accumulated weariness was catching up with her. But as she sat there in the half dark Judith wondered if she were not so much tired as she was disturbed—and for no good, sensible reason when she looked back on it.

It was ridiculous to let herself get worked up over Dow Slater—a perfect stranger. She was acting like some silly schoolgirl! He meant nothing to her—no more than just another customer who had happened to do her a favor, but still he was there, lodged deep in her mind and she could not keep from thinking about him.

There was something about him, a great strength yet a loneliness, or perhaps it was a bitterness that filled him, that reached out to her. It was as if he and the world had mutually rejected each other somewhere along the way and then discovering that no one finds fulfillment in isolation, was now striving to once more become a part of life.

That there was something in the past that troubled and grieved him, was certain. Undoubtedly it had some connection with his being a lawman and subsequently turning from that profession. It was equally certain that he did not wish to speak of it, for what little he had said, had come reluctantly.

And Glenna . . . She had set her sights on him right away, recognizing in him the sort of man who could do her a lot of good on that broken-down ranch she was so proud of. She'd use him in whatever way that suited her best with no thoughts as to his needs and feelings. It wouldn't surprise her one bit if, in a short time, Glenna dropped Ed Gault and centered her attentions on Slater. He'd make not only a good ranch foreman but a fine husband as well.

So what if Glenna did?

Judith stirred impatiently. It was no business of hers, and if Dow Slater liked the idea, so be it. Maybe that was what he wanted, was really searching for—a girl like Glenna Darrow with a ranch to offer along with herself.

A man such as he could never get interested in her, a

widow who ran a restaurant. That wouldn't be enough for him; he would have led an active, exciting life as a lawman and to expect him to settle down to the humdrum existence of a—what in heaven's name was she thinking of? A body would believe there was something between them! Why, she'd only met the man an hour or so ago!

But it was pleasant to think about him, to worry over him a little—and dream. As far as the restaurant was concerned she'd sell out in a minute if he ever asked her to, just as she'd go anywhere, do anything he wished. Not that the cafe hadn't been good to her; it had been her salvation after she lost Earl. But that was the past and ahead was the future, and it didn't count now—not if Dow Slater should ask her one day to make a choice.

"*Señora*—"

Teresa's soft voice came to her through the shadows, startled her. "Yes?"

"All is clean. I go home now."

"That's fine, Teresa . . . Good night."

"*Buenos noches, señora.*"

Judith heard the back door open, click shut. Rising, she crossed to the kitchen, passed through it to her living quarters in the rear. She wished now she had suggested to Dow that he drop back for a late cup of coffee, but it hadn't entered her mind. She could be sure Glenna Darrow would have thought of it, however.

7

Slater stepped out into the cool night. A few of the stores along the street were still open, their windows glowing with the pale sheen of lamplight, but the number of persons seen earlier along the walks had diminished greatly and he guessed Shibolem, except for its saloons, was about to call it a day. Pausing, he listened briefly to Judith Hazelwood moving about inside her place of business, and then continued on.

He realized he had enjoyed the evening. While there had been those few moments of distraction when he'd been forced to handle that drunk—Weber, Glenna Darrow had called him—the incident had not marred the occasion. It was good being in the company of a woman like Judith although her frankness had surprised him somewhat when they were speaking of Glenna. He wondered idly what lay between them. They appeared to rankle each other but each was careful to maintain a sort of icy neutrality. It could be Glenna; she had a driving way about her.

What would it be like to work for a woman, actually a mere slip of a girl? It would be a new experience and one he was not too sure he could live with for long, but he would give it a try. It meant having a job, something he needed for peace of mind as well as for his pocketbook. He'd go ahead, complete the chore she'd cut out for him, and then see how he felt.

He came to a halt in front of the Happy Jack Saloon, struck by the impulse to have a drink before he returned to Hurd's Livery Stable and a bed in its loft. Stepping up onto the porch, he crossed and entered.

A half a dozen men stood at the bar, perhaps twice that many were at tables set in a far corner playing cards. There was no one at the scarred and dusty piano, and the small area reserved for dancing was deserted. Evidently Happy Jack's competition, the Calico Girl, enjoyed the lion's share of the town's business.

"Whiskey," Slater ordered when the bartender moved up to him expectantly.

He was feeling the sweeping glances accorded him by the others in the room, brushed them off with a cool return look, and laying a coin on the counter, took up his drink. The aproned man behind the counter waited while he downed it, and then refilled the thick-bottomed shotglass at Dow's nod.

"Reckon you're the new ramrod at the Darrow place," he said, helping himself to a quarter from the change he had returned.

Slater nodded. "News gets around fast."

The barkeep's thick shoulders stirred. "Heard the deputy telling it to Joe Johnson. Your size, and when I seen you wasn't wearing iron—well, I figured you'd be him."

Dow considered the man in silence. Then: "You Happy Jack?"

"What I'm called. Mind me saying something personal?"

"Go ahead."

"Best you start packing iron if you aim to stay around here. Being big don't do you no good when there's a bullet coming your way."

"Truth in that," Slater agreed thoughtfully. "There some special meaning in it, too?"

The barman's solemn face did not change. "You keep thinking on what I said, that's all . . . Want another drink?"

Dow shook his head, reclaimed what was left of his dollar, and turned away. Apparently Tip Weber had been around mouthing threats—which was usually all such amounted to; the Tip Webers were most always loud talk and little else.

"Obliged," he said and started toward the door.

Happy Jack, engaged in mopping the counter with a damp cloth, did not look up. "There's a back way out of here if you're of a notion to use it."

Slater threw a side glance to the saloon's entrance. Shadowy figures moved about in the darkness beyond it. Weber had recruited some help if, as the saloonman seemed to think, he was waiting outside.

"Guess I am," Dow said, and following the direction of Happy Jack's nod, crossed the room to a door in the rear.

Opening it, he stepped out into an alley. Hurrying to the building's nearest corner, he stopped, listened briefly, and then doubled back to the street. Again he halted, at-

tention on several men loitering just outside the fan of
light spilling through the saloon's doorway.

One was Weber. Slater recognized him as he half
turned to speak to one of the others. He had been somewhere along the street evidently, and had seen him enter
Happy Jack's, Dow supposed. Now, with a few chosen
friends, he had arranged a reception.

A taut smile on his lips, and suddenly alive with the
old familiar throb of tension that sharpened his senses
and honed a sort of joyous anticipation within him, he
rounded the corner of the structure, and keeping in the
shadows lying close to the wall, crossed to where he was
standing unnoticed in the darkness directly behind
Weber.

"Ain't nobody shoving me around and getting away
with it," the puncher said. "No, by God! Ain't never let
nobody start, ain't about to now."

"You take my advice you'll forget it." It was Ben Denver, the rider who had been with Tip in Judith's. "Gun
or no gun that bird ain't somebody to be picking a fight
with."

"I can cut him down to size—"

"How'd it all start?" one of the other men asked.

"Me and Ben went in the widow's place aiming to grab
a bite of chow. Then this jasper just up and jumped me.
Was no call for it at all."

"You're not even a good liar," Slater said and stepped
out of the darkness.

Weber whirled. Slater's big hands caught him by the
shirt front. Jerking the man off his feet, he spun him

about, slammed him against the side of the saloon. Tip's breath exploded from his lungs in a gusty blast.

Holding the puncher upright with an extended arm, hand jammed against the throat, Dow threw a glance over his shoulder at Denver and the others.

"Stay out of this," he warned quietly, and knocking aside Weber's fingers frantically trying to reach the pistol on his hip, he drove a fist into the man's belly.

Weber groaned, buckled forward. Behind him Dow heard the crunch of gravel, took a hasty side step. Something smashed into the back of his neck. Arms went about his middle, seeking to drag him down.

Bracing himself, Slater caught Weber by a wrist, yanked him forward, and wheeling, threw him into the tight pack of Tip's friends, crowding in. As they stumbled away, he completed the turn, rocked backward, trapping the man clinging to him between his own body and the wall of the building. A yell of pain went up and the arms locked about him fell away.

Stepping clear of the man's flailing legs, Dow faded into the shadows, circled quickly to come in from behind on the confused milling of figures scrambling wildly to regain their footing. A shape loomed up before Dow. Putting his hands against the man's shoulders, Slater pushed hard. The man swore, and went stumbling back into the melee carrying several others down with him.

"Goddammit—let me get loose!"

Weber's exasperated shout cut through the grumbling and cursing. Dow, catching sight of the cowpuncher through the dust, stepped in swiftly. Tip had his pistol out and was struggling to get clear of the pile. Moving close, Slater swung his foot in a short arc. The toe of his boot caught the weapon from the side, sent it sailing off into the street.

A gunshot ripped through the welter of sounds. Ed Gault's voice shouted: "Be enough of this!"

Slater drew back, out of the flare of light. For the first time he saw that an audience had gathered on the porch of Happy Jack's, that others, hearing the scuffling, had come up from elsewhere along the street to watch.

The deputy, pistol in hand, swept the dusty, battered-looking cluster of men flanking Weber with a scornful glance.

"No reason for me to ask what this's all about or who started it," he said angrily. "Already know."

Weber, nursing his fingers, swore. "This ain't nothing for you to go butting into, Deputy. Between me and that damn drifter."

Gault smiled faintly. "More like between him and about half the town. Nevertheless, you ain't going to tear up my town trying to settle your scores. Try it again and I'll lock up the whole push of you. Hear?"

Slater heard Tip Weber mutter a reply, and turning away, started for the livery stable. He was suddenly worn, felt dusty and sweat soaked. A hot bath would be a treat but he knew he would have to forget that at least until morning and content himself with washing off at the water trough.

He slowed his steps, hearing the quick thump of boot heels in the half dark behind him.

"Hold up, Slater."

It was Gault's voice. Dow halted, turned to face the man. "Yeh?"

"Just aim to give you a bit of warning," the deputy said in a clipped sort of tone. "Trouble follows you around, seems, and your luck ain't going to hold out forever. You figure to stay alive around here you best start packing a gun. I reckon you know how to use one."

Dow Slater remained silent for a long breath, his eyes reaching out beyond the town to the dark sky bending overhead. Finally he nodded.

"Expect I do, Deputy," he said, and moved on.

8

Slater rose early, and after visiting the barber shop, presented himself at the Home Cafe where he enjoyed a hearty breakfast of eggs and bacon fortified with plenty of hot biscuits, jelly, and coffee. Judith was strangely quiet, not inclined to conversation, and when the meal was over he paid his check and returned to the livery stable. It was midmorning by then and saddling the sorrel, he rode out for the Darrow place.

He found himself in a disturbed state of mind as the big gelding loped easily along the well-traveled path. What was troubling Judith? Where that night before she had seemed warm, friendly, interested in him she was now cool and remote. What had brought about the change? Had she heard about the big ruckus he'd had with Tip Weber and his friends and had it somehow altered her opinion of him? Or did it have something to do with his going to work for Glenna Darrow for whom she obviously cared very little? He couldn't see why it should matter to her, but it was possible that it did.

And, too, he found himself recalling Deputy Ed Gault's words, and the thought came to him that he likely was taking on a task that could be better served by a man willing to use a gun if the need arose. But he had made it clear to Glenna that he no longer relied on a weapon and she had accepted him on that basis. Since it appeared to be so important she hire on a foreman capable of fulfilling the job's requirements, it was logical to assume she would have lost interest in him if she didn't think he could manage it.

Shaking off the nagging thoughts, he decided he'd leave it up to her. There was still time enough for her to change her mind—which she could very well do when he presented himself at the ranch and again made it plain that he was not signing on as a gunman. He'd give her to understand that he was willing to tackle the job she'd outlined for him but would do it his way. If she felt otherwise there'd still be time enough to call off the deal.

The Circle D was set back from the road a good quarter mile. The main house was a fairly large, slanted roof structure, once white but now showing a need for paint. Several lesser buildings, corrals, holding and branding pens lay beyond it and all was nestled in a cottonwood surrounded clearing.

To the east and south the land rolled away in gentle, grassy contours and well on in the west a low range of hazy blue mountains formed a backdrop. Fifty thousand acres of prime country made up the Darrow holdings; Hurd, the stable owner, had told him when he mentioned that he had found work on the Circle D. It was a shame that more hadn't been done with it.

Two women, a worthless boy and four old worn-out brush-jumpers whose main interest in life was eating and sleeping. If Glenna was smart she'd sell out to any one of the ranchers who'd be more than happy to take the place off her hands, and marry Ed Gault. Ed was a cinch to be the next sheriff, and after that—who knows—he could end up being the U. S. Marshal! Ed Gault was a climber!

Glenna and her mother were standing in the yard when Dow pulled up to the hitchrack. As the girl came forward to greet him she was smiling broadly.

"I'd begun to think you'd backed out on me!"

Slater pulled off his hat. "Said I'd be here and here I am. Point is, you still aim to hire me?"

"Of course," Glenna said, abruptly serious. Raising her hand she beckoned to several men standing in front of a long, low-roofed building on the opposite side of the hardpack.

Dow watched them move out, shamble toward him and the women . . . It was as he'd been told—four broken-down old cowhands. The Circle D was in a bad way, he thought ironically; a crew of has-beens ram-rodded by a man crippled by the past.

The cowhands drew to a halt in an uncertain line. Glenna nodded to them. "This is my new foreman, Dow Slater," she said, and after they had made a slight indication of acknowledgment, she pointed to the nearest, a sharp-faced balding man.

"This is Caleb Gore, Dow. He's been here longer than any of the others."

Slater took the old man's bony hand into his own, shook it. All wore pistols, he noted, but they looked to have gone unused for years.

"Aaron Kargill," Glenna continued, passing on to the next man.

Kargill was squat, a bit paunchy, had faded blue eyes, a thick beard and mustache.

"John Ledge—"

The third member of the Circle D crew was tall and emaciated with a skull-like face. What hair he still owned was red and his skin had a sort of mottled look, the result of endless years in the sun.

"Mighty pleased to know you, Slater," he said in an unmistakable Texas drawl.

"And this is Tom Farley."

Farley was of medium build, somewhat stooped but with quick, alert eyes. His grip was firm and while he did not appear to be any younger than his fellow ranchhands, he looked much stronger.

"Heard you had yourself quite a fandango in town last night with Tip Weber and his bunch," he said, bobbing approvingly. "Yes, sir, must've been quite a sociable!"

Dow shook his head, smiled. "Can't get over the way news travels in this country."

"Was Royce—Mister Darrow, told us. He seen it. The deputy, too—"

"Ed rode by early this morning," Glenna added. "We got it twice." She hesitated, looked at Slater closely. "Ed thinks you're a fool to be walking around without a gun."

"Told me that last night—or the same as."

"It doesn't change things?"

"No—"

Aaron Kargill's mouth sagged. He leaned forward, head outthrust on his wrinkled, turkey neck. "This ain't no put-on?"

Slater's features were stiff. "Gave up wearing a weapon a time back. Swore I'd never put one on again. Still mean to stand by that."

There was a long moment of shocked silence, and then Ledge said: "How the devil you figure to get by with that?"

"Guns you're packing don't look to me like they've been used in quite a spell—"

"That's a different horse. We ain't the kind to go around looking for trouble."

"And we sure ain't the ones that'll be heading up this here cattle drive the missy's planning on," Gore added. "How you going to work *that*?"

"If things go right," Glenna said slowly, "he won't need a gun."

"But there ain't no for-sure of that!" Kargill protested and swung his old eyes to Slater. "Maybe you'd be agreeing to carrying a rifle—or a scattergun?"

In the hush that followed the question Dow Slater looked out over the yard. A few steps away Mrs. Darrow stood quietly by, listening but taking no part in the conversation, just as she had done at Judith's.

"Like to get this straight. Happens I've done more than enough killing in my life and seen so much death there's nights when I don't sleep good. I've drawn the line on using a weapon—any kind and if I get killed someday because of that, I reckon it won't be a big loss.

"Big thing for you to understand is, I won't go back on my word to myself. If it's worrying any of you and you don't think I can do the job Miss Darrow's hiring me to do, now's the time to speak up."

Glenna frowned, touching each of the four men with her glance. She looked fresh and young in her riding togs and her skin had a warm, healthy glow. Beyond her Mrs. Darrow continued to stand by, hands folded, features placid. That she left all things up to her daughter was evident. He gave a moment's wonder as to the whereabouts of the third member of the family, Royce.

"Well, speak up! There any objections?"

Glenna's voice was a firm challenge. Slater realized at once that there was a side to the girl he had not yet become aware of.

"No, ma'am, only—"

"Only what?"

"It's the cattle drive we're worrying about," Kargill said. "Around the place we don't need no gun—and he won't neither. Expect, from what we heard, he can get by in town, too—but this here drive, that's something else."

"I expect to go into that with Slater," the girl said crisply, "let him know just what it's all about and what he'll be up against. If he still wants to go unarmed, it'll be his choice. It'll be different with you. You're wearing guns, and you'll keep right on wearing them."

John Ledge looked down at the weapon on his leg, an ancient Army Colt that had been converted from cap and ball to cartridge.

"'Spect we're doing that more from habit than anything else," he said ruefully. "Just ain't natural not to have my iron hanging on my leg. Sort've like wearing boots . . . I ain't even sure it'll fire."

"Best you find out," Glenna snapped. "That is, unless you want to sign the pledge and swear off guns like Slater has."

Dow's jaw hardened. He pushed back his temper. "Seems my way of living's going to be a problem. Smart thing for you to do is find somebody else."

"Don't make any decisions until you've heard what I've got to say," Glenna replied. "You need a job and I need a good man. It can be a one-shot deal, if you like. Once you've got my herd to the railhead and brought the money back to me, you can quit—or you can stay on as my foreman. Now, I figure you can get the job done —and whether you do it with or without a gun's up to you . . . Come on in the house and I'll lay it on the line. You can make up your mind then."

"It all right if we get back to the herd?" Kargill asked.

"Don't see as it makes much difference. There's nobody tending them most of the time anyway—but go on," the girl said. "I'll let you know how things stand soon as it's settled."

The men turned about, headed slowly for the bunkhouse. Glenna watched them for a moment, shook her head.

"I'd get rid of them faster than I can blink an eye if I had the cash to pay them off and hire on some good help."

"Glenna!" Mrs. Darrow exclaimed disapprovingly, speaking for the first time.

"Well, I would, Mama! They're too old to work. You know it same as I do—same as they do, and long as we have to depend on them we'll get nowhere!" Abruptly the girl whirled to face Slater. "That's why I hope you'll sign on, Dow. You can help me put this place back on its feet, make something good of it!"

"Already said I don't know much about cattle—"

"And I've said that's not important. It's getting over this first hump—making the drive to McCoy—that counts. Once that's done we've got the big problem licked . . . Come on. There'll be fresh coffee on the stove."

9

Glenna led the way into a back room of the house, a sort of boxed-in porch off the kitchen. A table and four chairs were in the center of the area and Slater guessed it was where the Darrows took their meals when the weather was agreeable.

"Sit down," the girl said in her direct, no-nonsense way. "I'll get the coffee."

Dow moved to a chair, hesitated as Mrs. Darrow entered, took a place at the table. As he settled onto the hard back, the elderly woman glanced at him shyly.

"Do you think you'll like it here, Mr. Slater?"

Evidently she was under the impression he had accepted the job as Circle D foreman or else had supreme confidence in her daughter's powers of persuasion. He shrugged.

"Expect so."

"I hope you will," she murmured and fell silent once more as Glenna came through the doorway with a mug of coffee in each hand. Noting her mother she frowned, placed the cups on the table and retraced her steps into the kitchen. Shortly she returned with a third container of the dark, steaming brew. Passing it to Mrs. Darrow, she sat down.

"Now maybe we can get down to business," she began. She paused and looked over her shoulder. An expression of annoyance again crossed her face as the screened panel opened and a young man entered.

Despite the different-colored eyes—blue instead of brown—the weak chin and loose mouth, it took but a glance for Slater to recognize him as the third member of the Darrow family.

"My brother, Royce," Glenna said, with an indifferent gesture. "This is Dow Slater, Royce."

Darrow nodded, said, "I've seen him," in a disinterested voice, and dragging one of the chairs into a corner of the room, sat down. Reaching into a pocket he drew forth a cigar, fired a match with a thumbnail, and cocking the chair on two legs against the wall, sucked the weed into life. Blowing a cloud of smoke into the air, he nodded.

"You folks go right ahead with your talking. I'll just listen."

Glenna studied him for a few moments, and then turned back to Slater. It was plain that Royce had already enjoyed a few drinks but he was not drunk.

"I think we can get on with it," she said.

Dow took a sip of his coffee. "Big thing's this cattle drive, I take it."

"Most important of all," Glenna agreed. "I'll be honest with you—nothing else really counts."

"How far is it to the railhead?"

"Ten days, more or less."

"Seems no big sweat. What's the rub?"

"It's the Hupperman Trail," Royce Darrow said. "That's the rub—and it's a big one."

Glenna flashed him an angry look. Not missing Darrow's veiled meaning, Slater put his attention back on the girl.

"There something about this Hupperman Trail I ought to know?"

"Yes, and I intended to tell you," she replied. "It's not the one used by other ranchers. They drive their herds east. Takes a month or more."

She paused, eyed him narrowly for reaction. Dow gave it thought, said, "But the trail east is safer, that it?"

"It is. Everybody around here used the Hupperman at one time, selling their beef at McCoy, but outlaws moved in and started raiding the herds. There's sort of a no man's land west of there, rough butte country, where they hang out. They'd stampede the herds, cut out a few hundred and drive them on to Mexico. The border's not very far south.

"Ranchers—my father was alive then—tried to do something about it, hired gunslingers, sent more trail hands with their herds, things like that, but it didn't help. Just got more men shot up. Ended up they quit driving their stock south over the Hupperman, sent them east instead. Been that way now for several years."

"Outlaws still use it as a hangout?" Slater asked.

"Far as we know but they won't be expecting anybody to be bringing a herd through. Chances are you won't run into any of them."

"Can't move cattle without raising dust. I'd say the

chances were pretty good . . . Looks to me like you'd be better off to drive your stock east along with the other ranchers."

"I can get ten dollars more a head by not throwing in with the rest and making my own drive to McCoy instead. There'll be four hundred steers in the herd and that works out to four thousand extra dollars in my pocket."

Evidently there was some reason why cattle brought more at McCoy than at the railhead to the east, but Slater guessed it was no business of his. And for an additional ten dollars for each beef he could understand why Glenna, in desperate straits, was willing to gamble. For her it had come down a win-big or lose-all proposition.

But why was she so insistent on choosing him to boss the drive? He'd made it clear he had only a slight acquaintance with cattle, and that he would not break his determination to go unarmed. Since the herd would be moving through country known to be plagued with outlaws and rustlers, it seemed only common sense to employ men willing to use guns.

"Still got me wondering why you picked me for this job—knowing how I feel."

Glenna shrugged her small shoulders. "You hit town looking for a job, I had one open and—"

"Tell him the truth," Royce Darrow said. "You can't find anybody else that's fool enough to take it."

The girl flushed slightly. "Oh, I expect I could if I had the time and tried hard enough. Fact is, I've got to get the steers to McCoy as soon as possible."

Dow finished the last of his coffee, stared off through the open doorway into the yard. The area was deserted except for several chickens wandering aimlessly about along the edge of the hardpack.

He reckoned he had the story now. Glenna, badly needing cash, and set on proving herself, could accomplish both by selling her cattle at the nearest railhead—a point reached only by driving the stock through outlaw-infested country. She could find no one else willing to undertake the chore, and encountering him, a stranger, and perhaps impressed by his handling of Tip Weber, had made him an offer.

"Not sure I want to take the deal either," he said.

Glenna bit at her lower lip. "I'll double the pay, make it a hundred dollars—"

"That's not important. It's that you folks will be depending on me, and with the kind of odds I'll be up against I don't figure I'd be smart to take on the responsibility."

Glenna cast a look at Royce. His head had dropped forward, and chin sunk in his chest, he was beginning to doze.

"Here's something that'll cut down the odds a bit," she said in a low voice. "Nobody knows about it and I want it kept that way. The Army's there."

"The Army?"

Glenna made a quick, cautioning gesture with a forefinger, threw a hasty glance at her brother. Royce Darrow appeared to be asleep.

"Yes. They've set up camp about ten miles this side of

McCoy. They'll have patrols working the country right along. It'll make a difference—the outlaws'll stay clear of the Trail."

"Should. Where'd you hear about the Army?"

The girl nodded at Mrs. Darrow. "The colonel in charge is an old admirer of Mama's. She got a letter from him telling her about the post and saying he'd like to pay a call."

A ghost of a smile pulled at Slater's lips. "And nobody else knows about it?"

"No one, not even Royce—only my mother and me. And like I've said, I want it kept quiet. If it got out all the rest of the ranchers in the valley would start driving beef to McCoy, and the price I can get, spot cash, for my steers, would go to hell."

Slater's grin widened. Glenna Darrow was quite a woman. She was willing to play the role of a foolish girl sending her herd on a drive through country where outlaws were known to operate freely, with a trail boss that lacked all of the usual requirements and a crew barely able to do a day's work, knowing all the while that she was holding aces.

More or less under the protection of the Army, the chances of completing the drive with no losses to the outlaws were better than good, and when it was over she would have the laugh on everybody.

"That make it sound a bit easier?" he heard her ask.

"Makes a difference, all right . . . I hear you say something about getting paid off in cash? Four hundred steers'll bring quite a bit of—"

"Eight thousand dollars at twenty a head. You'll collect cash—no bank draft. I've already made the deal with the buyer. Reason is I don't want everybody in town knowing just how much money we'll have. With a draft going into the bank it'd be all over town in no time."

Slater nodded. He could attest as to the speed with which news circulated in the area. "Lot of cash to be carrying."

"I realize that and I wouldn't handle it this way if it wasn't absolutely necessary. The Circle D owes a lot of money and if I met all our debts we'd have nothing left over to start building up the ranch with. Long as nobody knows for sure what we got, I can satisfy the creditors with part payment . . . Anyway, I think I've got a little help going there for you, too. Ed Gault's agreed to go along on the drive. And, of course, Royce will be with you."

Dow glanced at the sleeping man. He doubted if Darrow could stay sober long enough to be of much use but Gault, a lawman, would be an asset.

"I figure to give you three of the crew," Glenna continued. "With Ed, Royce, and yourself, there'll be six of you. Ought to be enough to handle four hundred head with no trouble."

Slater shrugged. "You're a better judge of that than me . . . What kind of country is it, rough?"

"Not specially. Mostly flats with the buttes and brakes over to the west. Grass will be real good and there's a river, not a very big one but with plenty of water in it, that you'll crisscross several times."

"Drive out to be pretty much a cinch—"

"Then you're taking the job?"

"I'm ready to start any time," Slater said, glancing at Royce. The cigar had fallen from his fingers, lay on the floor. He was snoring softly, hat tipped forward over his eyes. The sphinx-like Mrs. Darrow, smiled faintly with her eyes, continued to stare off into the yard.

"Good. I've got most of the arrangements made. You can figure on moving the herd out in the morning. It will be Ledge, Farley, and Kargill going with you. I'm looking for Ed Gault to drop by any minute so I'll tell him . . . Now, if there's anything you need, personal I mean, go to Tilton's and have it put on my bill. We can settle up when I pay you off. That suit you?"

Dow nodded. "Can use a few things. Doubt if the pants I'm wearing would last through a day's hard riding."

"If Tilton doesn't have what you want, go over to Turner's. We've got a bill there, too." Glenna hesitated, met his level gaze frankly. "About a gun—you sure you're not being foolhardy, feeling the way you do about carrying one? For your own sake, I mean . . . Now, if you want to change your thinking, I'll stake you to a new outfit at Bud Mason's gunshop—"

"Obliged, but I'll manage," Slater said coolly, getting to his feet. He was growing a little weary of people trying to hang a weapon on him. Only Judith seemed to understand. "There anything I can do toward getting things lined up?"

"No, what's left the crew and I can handle."

"See you first off in the morning, then," Dow said, and

nodding to the girl and her mother, stepped out into the yard and crossed to his horse.

He should hang around the ranch, get better acquainted and do what he could to get set for the drive, he supposed, in spite of what Glenna Darrow had said, but he had an urge to see and talk with Judith once more.

10

Entering town, Dow Slater rode first to Tilton's General Store and there outfitted himself with socks, a change of drawers, a new pair of pants, and a shirt. The boots and hat he wore would do, at least for the time being. Making the change in the rear of the establishment, he stored the extra items in his saddlebags and made his way to the Home Cafe.

Judith was in the kitchen when he stepped through the doorway. It was past noon and there were no customers. At the rap of his heels she appeared, a smile quickly parting her lips.

He grinned, swept off his hat. "Wasn't sure you'd recognize me, all spruced up like I am."

She came on into the room, features abruptly sober. "I guess this means you took the job at Darrows and will be making that cattle drive."

Slater nodded. "It's not going to be as bad as you figured," he said, taking a chair at one of the tables. He wished he could tell her about the Army encampment, and thus reassure her; the secret would be safe with her he was certain, but he was reluctant to have her involved in the event the information was leaked by another source.

"You don't know that," she said heavily, pausing to get coffee and cups.

He watched her move up to the table, sit down opposite and fill the container she'd placed before him. Judith seemed genuinely disturbed and it pleased him to know she worried about him a little. The persons who had cared about him to any extent throughout his life could be counted on one hand with a finger or two to spare.

"I heard some men talking about it in here this morning," she continued. "They think Glenna's a fool to try and get her cattle to McCoy, that she ought to go ahead, turn her stock over to some other rancher, let him drive them to the east railhead along with his, the same as before."

Slater gave that thought. "Wondered how she'd been handling it," he said. "Things could be different on this trail to McCoy now. I figure I can make it all right."

"Glenna's got you believing that, but you don't really know what you'll be up against. The cattlemen had to give up that railhead years ago. It was just too costly, too dangerous."

"There'll be six of us making the drive, three of her crew, the deputy, Ed Gault, and her brother—"

Judith sniffed. "A lot of help Royce'll be! And far as her crew is concerned—they're good old men but that's just it—they're old."

Masking a smile, Slater took a swallow of coffee, said, "And the deputy?"

"You won't be able to depend on him much either. It's my guess he'll run at the first sign of trouble. He's not going to take any chances on missing out being the next sheriff."

"There something wrong between you and Glenna Darrow?" Dow asked after a time. There was a faint thread of amusement in his tone.

"It takes a woman to know a woman," she answered.

"Now, what's that mean?"

"Means that I know Glenna for what she is—a schemer who's thinking only of herself. She'll use you, Dow, and she won't give a rap what it costs you or anybody else. If you get yourself killed trying to get her cattle to Mc-Coy—too bad. She won't lose a wink of sleep over it and it's not in her to ever be sorry."

"I don't kill off easy—"

"What chance will you have? You don't go armed, and I admire you for refusing to do so, but how can you protect yourself and stay alive?"

"Been plenty of other men able to live without packing a gun. I figure I can make it, too."

"But did any of them take a job driving cattle through country everybody else avoided because of outlaws?"

"Expect some of them took on jobs that were just as risky," he said, impatience stirring within him.

He hadn't come in for a lecture on what he should and should not do but to see approval in Judith's eyes. Somewhere along the way since his arrival in Shibolem, it had become important to know that he pleased her; instead he was getting only criticism.

"You reckon we could talk about something else?"

Judith sighed, lowered her eyes. "I'm sorry. It's none

of my business, I know—it's just that I hate to see Glenna use you."

"I'm past the growing-up time. I know what she's doing and it's all right with me. Far as the risks go, could be things've changed along this Hupperman Trail, as they call it. Want you to trust me . . . Now, you got any of that peach pie left?"

"Today it's apple. Will it do?"

"Be fine," Slater said, and reached for the pot of coffee as Judith rose, moved off toward the kitchen.

Filling his cup, Dow twisted about, looked off into the street. Deputy Ed Gault was in conversation with two men in front of Johnson's Feed Store. A small boy with a puppy clutched tight in his arms, was hurrying on short legs for the houses that stood beyond the town's business district. A quiet, sleepy peacefulness lay over the settlement, a sort of lethargy that set a man at ease with all things—and himself.

The dark days seemed far behind him now, the dragging, empty hours in which he had wandered aimlessly on, mind in torment, the past a bitter recollection, the future a gray void. Those moments in Powderville were still a vivid memory entrenched in a shadowy corner of his mind—the screams, the vision of a woman's tortured face, the blast of guns, and the drifting, stinging powder smoke—it was all there, but no longer was it foremost; now it had to be recalled to be relived.

He had thought the recollection of those terrible, flaming seconds would never fade but stay etched permanently in his eyes, and that he would carry such to his grave. He was finding it not so, that there was a life to be had beyond that memory, one that had slowly begun to unfold when he rode into a town called Shibolem and saw a welcome in the smile of Judith Hazelwood.

And Glenna Darrow . . . He owed much to her, also. No doubt she was selfish, a schemer and dead-set on having her own way at any cost, but she had been willing to give him a job on his terms although she had made it clear she thought him foolish, his attitude outlandish in a land where all men went armed.

Neither of the women nor any of the men he'd encountered had made any determined effort to pry out the reasons why he felt as he did, and he was grateful for that. It would be difficult for him, a lawman of long standing, to explain what had taken place inside him at Powderville, and he hoped the time would never come when he'd be compelled to recount the incident. It would be like going through hell and, like as not, before he'd let himself in for such, he'd walk away and let it be. He could think of no reason important enough to make it necessary.

The deputy and his friends parted, the lawman pointing for his office, the men angling purposefully for Happy Jack's Saloon. He could drop by, tell Gault that he had hired on at the Circle D and planned to move out the herd that next day, he supposed, but Glenna had said she would make it known to him. Best leave it at that; she could have a reason for handling it herself.

Somewhere along the street iron clanged against iron as a blacksmith began to work at his anvil, and back and to the west of the buildings, he heard the hollow beat of a running horse.

"Sorry it took so long." Judith's voice brought him around suddenly. "I wanted to heat it."

She placed the wedge of pie before him. A large chunk of butter was melting slowly on the crust, and taking his fork, Slater spread it evenly over the golden-brown, flaky surface.

"When will you be leaving?" she asked.

"Tomorrow—early. We're all set to go according to Glenna."

"She's been ready for a week or more," Judith said drily. "Just couldn't find a man who'd hire on and take the—"

Slater glanced up. There was a flatness in his eyes and the planes of his face were drawn tight.

Judith shook her head apologetically. "I—I'm sorry. It's none of my business, I know, but I just can't be happy over your doing this."

"I'll be all right. It's only a job—and there's something I guess I've got to prove to myself."

"That you don't need a gun?"

His thick brows lifted betraying his surprise at her perception. "I'm trying to live without one. Not sure I can. Good chance someday something will happen and I'll just turn back to the old ways before I realize what I'm doing."

"Then you shouldn't be making this cattle drive for the Darrows. There's bound to be trouble . . . Why not find a job where there'll be no danger of ever having to use a weapon?"

"I'm no hand at taking the easy way out," he said, shrugging. "I'd rather know where I stand with myself now."

Judith fell silent, and then when he had finished the pastry and rose to go, she laid a hand on his arm.

"I hope you find out," she said quietly, "and I'll be praying that it will be the way you want it."

His mouth pulled back into a taut smile. "Obliged. Reckon I'll be needing your prayers—right along with a lot of luck . . . So long."

Royce Darrow, sitting at a table in a back corner of the Calico Girl, glanced up as the saloon's swinging doors opened. It was Ed Gault, and raising a hand, he called, "Over here, Sheriff!"

At once the lawman threaded his way through the scatter of empty chairs and unused tables toward Darrow. What few customers were present at that hour were at the bar or on the opposite side of the big room where several of the girls were lounging about.

"Toby Gates said you wanted to see me," the lawman began, and then centered his attention on the bottle of whiskey in Darrow's hand. "When're you going to start laying off that rotgut? I ain't seen you full sober in six months."

Royce, with a bland smile, lifted the bottle, took a deliberate swallow, and then offered it to Gault. "Good for what ails a man. Have a snort."

The deputy shook off the invitation, settled onto one of the chairs. "What'd you want to see me about?" he demanded impatiently.

"Talked to Glenna since this morning?"

"Nope, headed out that way now."

"Well, I just figured I ought to tell you she hired on that jasper—Slater. He's moving the herd out in the morning."

Gault shrugged. "I figured she'd talk him into it."

"We're expected to go along with him . . . You promise her you would?"

"Did say something like that a while back when she first got the idea. Was before this Slater came along."

"Well, she ain't going to let you forget it," Darrow said, taking another drink.

Gault swore quietly. "Just never thought somebody'd show up that'd be fool enough to take on the job. Reckon there's nothing I can do but stand by my word."

"Nope, guess not—but you'll be cutting your own throat if he makes it. Think you ought to know that."

The lawman frowned. "What're you getting at?"

"Just something I heard Glenna tell Ma. Said that this Slater was the kind of man she'd sure like to have around, and if that means what I think it does you're apt to find yourself standing out in the cold. You know Glenna. When she sets her cap for something she usually ends up getting it."

Gault stared. "That drifter? Who the hell you trying to josh? He don't mean nothing to her—never will."

Royce settled back on his chair, tipped his hat lower

over his eyes. "Could be. Just thought I'd best warn you
. . . Sure you don't want a drink?"

Ed Gault got slowly to his feet, a deep frown on his
face. "No, not right now," he murmured, turning for the
door. "See you later."

"Expect you will," Darrow agreed, and took another
pull at the bottle.

11

In spite of previous preparations it was midafternoon that next day before they got the herd underway. It was a late hour to start, Slater knew, but he felt that to just get the drive started would be a gain, and so with much grumbling from Kargill, Ledge, and Farley, the three cowhands assigned to him, and a noticeable lack of interest in the operation on the part of Royce, they moved the steers out. Glenna, who accompanied them for a short distance, advised him that Ed Gault would join them later.

They made perhaps five miles before sunset overtook them, and bedded down the herd for that first night in a deep swale lush with sweet grass. The girl had been correct in saying they would encounter no grazing problem since the Hupperman Trail had not been used by drovers in years; the way it was shaping up it was likely that Circle D steers would be the only ones in history to add tallow during a drive rather than lose it.

The meal that night was a quiet one, being mostly grub prepared by the Darrow cook and stored away in sacks and cans. Dow had agreed that the duration of the drive was too brief to bother with a chuck wagon, thus two pack horses were outfitted to carry supplies. The cooking chores, which would be few, were taken on by Aaron Kargill who, by his own words, volunteered mainly because he couldn't stand to drink anyone else's coffee.

The cattle were restless, as was to be expected, and Slater and his crew found themselves almost constantly on the move, circling the animals, drifting through them, comforting and soothing them by their presence. Toward morning a storm broke out over the distant mountains, and while there was much flashing of lightning and deep, rolling thunder, it was too far off to greatly disturb the steers.

Morning finally came, and after a breakfast of flapjacks, side meat, and boiled coffee, they got the herd on the way again, moving due south and down the center of a wide valley. He quickly discovered there was little point in asking questions of Royce Darrow or the crew relative to the country they were entering. Darrow kept wholly to himself, usually on the far side of the herd, nursing a quart fruit jar of whiskey; the elderly cowhands maintained a sullen aloofness, giving only resentful, monosyllabic replies to the queries put to them. As a result Slater, positioning the men around the herd at drag, swing, and lead, rode on ahead to see for himself.

If the country did not change drastically, it should be an easy drive, he saw as he looked out over the rolling land. Grass was evident as far as the eye could reach and while no river was yet visible, he knew they would come to water that next day if all went well. He should bear steadily south for the first fifty miles or so and then veer slightly eastward, Glenna had told him. Such would keep

the cattle well away from the buttes favored by the outlaws and take him on a more or less direct line to McCoy.
The Army encampment would lie somewhere in between.

The herd trailed well, after once settling down, and
an old brindle steer, electing himself leader and forging
to the front, made their job much easier. By the time
darkness again was upon them and a halt was made, they
had covered a good distance.

But with the arrival of sundown came also the departure of Royce Darrow. He had simply ridden off with a
wave of his hand and the shouted word that he would
see them in McCoy. Dow Slater had a better understanding of Glenna at that moment; the welfare of the
Circle D meant nothing to Royce, thus the entire responsibility for the ranch fell upon her shoulders.

"Don't see that it matters none," Aaron Kargill said,
as they squatted about a low fire eating the evening meal.
"That boy's about as handy as a wart on the end of a
man's nose, anyway."

"The truth," Ledge muttered, and glanced over at
Slater. "Thought you said the deputy was going to be riding with us."

"Was told he would be," Dow replied.

"Well, he's mighty slow showing up," the man
mumbled.

They had little confidence in him, Dow had soon
realized, chiefly because he went unarmed, and knowing their own limitations with the weapons they carried,
they were worried. Now, with Royce Darrow gone and

Gault's failure to put in a promised appearance, their situation would be critical should outlaws attack.

"How's it come you're so dead sot against packing iron?" Ledge asked peevishly. "You sure don't look like no psalm-singing galoot that's a-scared of using a gun."

Slater shook his head. "Was a time when I wouldn't walk across a street without a weapon hanging on my hip. I changed."

"Changed—why?" Kargill demanded, digging into a pocket for pipe and tobacco.

Dow Slater's face was impassive, and the firelight flickering upon it gave him a lean, remote look. After a moment he shrugged, took a swallow from the tin cup he was holding.

"Reckon that's his business," Farley said when it became apparent no answer was coming. "And if he ain't of a mind to talk about it, that's his business, too."

Far off to the west a wolf howled at the starlit sky. Kargill, the charred bowl of his briar filled, reached for a burning brand, held it to the tobacco and puffing the pipe into life, listened briefly to the sound.

"You maybe a gunhawk once?" he continued, ignoring Tom Farley's admonition.

"Lawman," Slater said. Tossing away the remaining dregs of coffee in the cup, he got to his feet. "We'll be getting into short hill country tomorrow. I want to keep the herd on the low ground. Less chance of them being seen. Keep them off the sand flats, too. Don't want to raise any more dust than we have to."

"Best you do your talking to that old brindle," Ledge said drily. "It's him that's doing the leading."

"I'll be riding point," Dow replied. "I'll keep him headed right."

"Well, come tomorrow, I sure hope that deputy shows up," Farley said. "We're drawing close to trouble and could be we'll be needing him bad."

"Maybe not. Word of the drive's been kept quiet. Not many folks know about it."

"Hell," Kargill said in disgust. "Everybody in the whole damn valley knowed the Darrows was going to make this drive to McCoy."

"Expect that's so—but they didn't know when. Way I understand it the herd's been ready for some time but they didn't have a trail boss. Far as most folks know the girl's still trying to find one."

"Meaning what?"

"There's a good chance we can get pretty far along before the word gets out, and if we keep clear of the buttes and hold down the dust, like as not we'll make it to McCoy without any trouble."

"Something I reckon you're right anxious to dodge, not been fixed to meet it. What happens if a bunch of them rustlers pays us a call? We light out for home?"

There was heavy sarcasm in Aaron Kargill's tone. Dow pushed back the temper rising within him. "We'll cross the creek when we come to it—if we do," he said coldly.

John Ledge shrugged, reached for a handful of dry brush and tossed it into the fire. At once the flames leaped upward, lighting the area.

"Ain't going to be no picnic," he drawled. "Man sure can't hide no four hundred steers and there ain't nothing that'll keep them quiet—bawling and bellyaching the way they like to do . . . And dust—kicks up even if they're walking in hock-deep grass. There just ain't nothing we can do to keep from getting spotted."

Kargill swore, tapped the dottle from his pipe against the heel of his boot. "I was against this from the start. The little gal'd been a lot better off to throw these here steers in with them other ranchers', let them trail them east for her same as always. She'd a drawed less money but she'd a got it. Now, with this fool stunt like as not she won't be getting nothing."

The wolf howled again into the night, the sound distant and lonely. Slater guessed he could expect little else from the Circle D crew. He was unknown, a stranger and an odd one at that who refused to carry a gun. That in itself marked him as a man from whom little could be expected . . . Perhaps they were right. Maybe he was a fool to have undertaken the job feeling as he did. He could . . .

A dry branch snapped in the darkness beyond the edge of firelight. Slater pivoted swiftly as the others came to sharp attention. Three figures moved into the pale glow . . . Tip Weber, with a friend at each shoulder.

12

"What the hell you birds doing here?" Tom Farley demanded, coming to his feet.

Slater raised a hand, waved back the older man. "Looking for me, I expect," he said quietly.

Weber nodded. "You guessed right," he said, and thumbs hooked in his belt, moved deeper into the circle of light.

The pair with him looked vaguely familiar to Dow. He guessed they had been among those with Tip that night in front of Happy Jack's.

"Heard in town you'd took off for McCoy with a bunch of the Darrows' cows. Had to ride right smart to catch up," Weber said, coming to a spraddle-legged halt.

"So—"

"Figured it'd be a good time to sort of square up things—us out here by ourselves where there won't be nobody butting in . . . I see you still ain't wearing a gun."

Slater shook his head.

"Well, I'll give you your choosings. It's going to be guns or fists. Either you strap on some iron and we'll settle it with lead, or I'm going to hammer you up so bad you won't be no good for nothing, for a week of Saturdays!"

Farley laughed. "From what I heard you didn't do so good trying it the other night."

"Never you mind, Grandpa," Weber replied coldly. "I wasn't back of the barn when the brains was passed out. I know when I'm overmatched. Reason I brung Pike and Jace with me."

Ledge swore. "You saying all three of you aim to jump on him?"

"Just what I am—they'll be doing the holding while I work him over . . . How about it, Mister Slater? You want to try outdrawing me or are we going—"

"Forget the guns," Dow cut in harshly, measuring the men with his eyes. Pike and Jace were big, husky, and he'd have small chance of breaking free of them once they locked their hands onto him. But he certainly didn't intend to take a bad beating from Tip Weber—and avoiding both would call for care on his part . . . Abruptly a thought slipped into his mind, one that came easily, stealthily. Why not—for just this one time—go back to the old ways and use a gun? He could save time, trouble and undoubtedly spare himself a lot of pain. It would be easy, so easy to rid himself of Weber—the others, too, if they tried to cut in.

"What's eating you, anyway?" Tip wondered, his voice filled with disgust. "You just a plain yellowback?"

Slater's eyes were flat, empty. A whiteness showed along the edge of his jaw, and then the tenseness that had gripped him eased as he pushed the impulse gripping him aside, deliberately filled his mind with a different thought . . . He'd best warn the crew to keep a sharper watch over the herd now. Weber had mentioned hearing the drive was underway; others would also be aware of such. That being a fact his hoped for passage for a few days without drawing attention was lost . . .

"All right, you had your chance," Weber was saying. "Can't nobody ever say I wasn't fair about this . . . Jace, why don't you de-horn them old codgers and throw their irons off into the bushes. Don't want them getting any cute ideas."

The heavier of Weber's sidekicks moved in close. One by one he relieved Kargill and the others of their weapons and tossed them into the circle of dark brush. Finished, he bucked his head at Tip.

"Reckon we can start the ball anytime—"

Weber grinned tightly, unbuckled his gunbelt and let it fall to the ground. Gloved hands chafing each other, he threw a glance at the Circle D crew, gathered in a silent cluster on the opposite side of the fire.

"Stay put. Try cutting in and you'll get some of what your friend's going to get . . . All right, boys, grab him!"

As the two men moved toward him, Slater bent low. Scooping up a handful of ashes, he flung it into the face of the man called Pike. Clawing at his eyes, the rider howled, staggered back. Instantly Dow rushed by him, threw himself into Weber. The blast of Jace's pistol jolted the night into echoes, brought a frantic yell from Weber, going down hard under Slater's weight.

"Don't shoot—goddammit! You'll hit me!"

Dow, sledging a fist into Tip's jaw, jerked clear as Jace, holstering his weapon, closed in, big arms outstretched.

Batting them away Slater went flat on the ground, rolled to the side. His right hand came in contact with Weber's discarded gunbelt. Grasping it, he leaped upright, and holding the heavy, cartridge filled strap by the buckle, he swung it at Jace.

The pistol fell from its holster as the belt arced through the dusty air. Dow felt it underfoot as the strap caught Jace on the side of the head, felled him like an axed steer.

Nearby Weber had scrambled to his feet. Cursing, he yelled for Pike to move in, to use his gun as he sought to avoid the cartridge belt Slater continued to swing in a whistling circle.

Abruptly Dow let go of the strap. It struck Pike high on the chest, sent him stumbling back. He tripped, went down, and as Slater wheeled to face Weber, he heard Tom Farley's joyous shout.

"Pile onto him, boys! The other'n, too! Let's keep this 'tween the boss and Tip!"

Dow grinned faintly. *The boss.* He guessed he'd finally broken down their skepticism and resentment. A fist jarred him free of further thoughts. Weber, head down, arms working like pistons, was crowding in on him. He pulled back, took a flurry of blows in the belly, and then linking his hands into a single fist, brought them down on the back of the man's neck.

Weber went to his knees. Stunned, he hung there for several seconds, finally began to draw himself upright. Dow, showing no mercy, swung a long uppercut. His knuckled hand connected with the point of Tip's chin.

The force of the blow raised the man off the ground, stretched him out full length on his back.

Heaving for breath, Slater turned about. Kargill was adding fuel to the scattered fire. Beyond him Tom Farley and Ledge were standing over Pike and Jace, who, with pistols pointed at their heads, showed no inclination to continue the fight.

"Get some rope," Dow said huskily. "We'll truss them up, turn them over to the deputy when he gets here. As soon they'd not be running loose and maybe be waiting for us somewhere down the trail."

Kargill hurried off at once to where the horses were picketed, returned shortly with several strips of rawhide. Saying nothing, he tossed a length to each of his partners and knelt beside Weber. Rolling the man over, he bound Tip's wrists together. By the time he was through, Ledge and Farley had secured Jace and Pike.

"Good place over there by them rocks to stash them," Kargill said, pointing to a ragged pile of weeds and boulders at the edge of the fire's light. "Won't be underfoot there and I sure ain't anxious to have them for company."

Grasping Tip by the collar, he dragged the slowly recovering man to a standing position, pushed him roughly toward the mound. Ledge and Farley prodded their prisoners to Weber's side, and when all three had been further restricted by roping their feet together, the old men, flushed and grinning, returned to the fire.

"Reckon that'll hold them!" Ledge said, rubbing his

hands together. "Mister, the way you rousted them about was a sight for sore eyes!"

"For a fact," Kargill added, holstering his retrieved pistol. "Sure figured we was in for trouble when they showed up fixing to take you apart—"

Slater was only half listening, his gaze on the shadows beyond the camp. "Somebody else's out there," he said quietly.

Almost immediately a hail came from the darkness. "Hello—the camp! It's Ed Gault!"

Slater breathed easier. Thoughts of outlaws, of rustlers had swept through his mind. They would have been caught off guard and completely unprepared.

"Come on in," he answered, and turned to Ledge and the others. "From here on we watch the herd closer."

"You thinking about that bunch that hangs around the buttes?"

Slater nodded, eyes on the deputy swinging off his horse at the edge of the camp. How long had Gault been out there in the darkness?

"Was hoping we could get a bit nearer to McCoy before anybody much knew we were on the trail. Can forget that now. Those outlaws likely've got friends in town— and if Tip Weber caught wind of the drive, they did, too."

"That's a sure bet," Farley said. "What do you want us to do?"

"Take your blankets and bed down close to the herd— one of you on each flank, third man out front. I'll work from here." Slater paused. Gault had stopped at the mound of rocks, was looking down at Weber and his two friends. He appeared to be saying something to them. "I'll be making rounds every couple of hours or so 'til first light."

"What's been going on here?" the lawman asked, coming on into the flare of light. "They give you some trouble?"

"Tried," Slater replied. "Want you to take them back to town, lock them up for a spell."

Gault brushed back his hat, scratched at his head. "Can't hardly do that—leastwise not without a charge of some kind."

Kargill snorted angrily. "Charge! They come sneaking in here all set to start a ruckus. When Slater there wouldn't draw on Tip, all three of them jumped him, aiming to beat him up! Just happens they got more'n they bargained for."

"Shooting off a gun, too," Ledge added. "Could've caused a stampede if them cows'd been edgy. I seem to recollect there's a law about that."

The deputy nodded. "Yeh, expect that'll do. I'll lay over for the night, head back for town in the morning with them . . . Any coffee left in that pot?"

"Help yourself," Dow said as Kargill and the others circled the fire, moving off for their horses. "You riding all the way with us?"

"What I'd planned," Gault replied, pouring himself a cup of the thick, black liquid. "This'll change things a mite, however—going back to town."

"Slow as we'll be moving you won't have any problem catching up."

The deputy took a swallow of the coffee, grimaced, said, "No, reckon not. Where's Royce?"

"Took off for McCoy."

Gault emptied his cup onto the ground, shrugged. "Might've known . . . Everything else going along all right?"

"Fine," Slater said, turning away. "Got to get set for the night. Some extra blankets there by my bedroll. Help yourself."

Moving on, he crossed to where the horses stood in their rope corral and mounted his sorrel. The crew had already ridden out, were by that time at their assigned positions.

Circling the herd, resting quietly in the deep grass, Slater fixed the locations of his three men in his mind, and an hour later, doubled back to the camp. Ed Gault had made himself comfortable near the fire which he had replenished and was sleeping soundly. Farther over at the mound of rocks, Weber, with Jace and Pike slumped beside him, called out angrily.

"How about a couple of them blankets for us? Getting cold laying here."

Taking a pair of the woolen covers, Dow carried them to where the men lay, spread them crosswise over their bodies, and making no comment, returned to the fire. There, crawling into his bedroll, he dropped off to sleep almost immediately.

He awoke a short time later, and again mounting, made

his slow check. Kargill, Ledge, and Farley were in their places and he passed them by at a distance, careful not to arouse them. It wasn't necessary for the crew to remain awake, only that they be near the herd at different points in the event trouble erupted. He had assumed for himself the chore of periodically patrolling the herd.

Satisfied that all was well, Slater cut back to camp. Gault was sleeping soundly in the dying glow of the flames, and continuing on, he swung the sorrel up to the rope enclosing their small remuda, and dismounted, weariness now beginning to drag at him.

He drew up sharply. The horses that Weber, Jace and Pike were riding, and that had been picketed nearby, were gone. Wheeling, he threw his glance to the mound of weedy rocks. The men were also missing.

13

Slater swore harshly, trotted to the pile of rocks. The blankets he'd thrown over the men lay in a heap to one side. Bits of the tough, rawhide cord used to bind their wrists were scattered about on the ground. The rope that bound their feet had also been slashed, was now in several short lengths. He looked toward the fire. Kargill had placed the weapons the men had carried near his blanket roll; the pistols, together with Weber's belt and holster, were no longer there.

Puzzled, Slater walked slowly into the circle of fading light. It was difficult to understand how the men could have freed themselves. True, none of them had been searched for a knife—he hadn't felt it necessary. A man with his hands linked tightly together would find it hard to extract his blade from a pocket and make use of it. But one of the three had, somehow, and they had made good an escape, probably shortly after he had ridden out that second time to look over the herd.

Halting, he stood for a few moments studying the sleeping deputy. Moving about quietly Tip and his partners would not have disturbed the lawman, thus he could in no way be blamed. Shrugging, Dow took up his blanket, and draping it about his shoulders to ward off the chill, sat down to consider what lay ahead where Weber was concerned.

It was senseless, of course, to awaken Gault and attempt to find the three men. They could be hiding somewhere in the darkness waiting for another opportunity to settle the score with him—or they could have given it up and headed back to Shibolem, or possibly some other town if they thought the deputy would start a search for them.

It was wiser, he finally concluded, to just let matters ride. The chances were good that Tip Weber would forget his desire for vengeance, at least until some later time —probably after the drive was over and they happened to come face to face by accident on a dark street. But should Tip persist, and circling ahead, be waiting in ambush along the trail, the presence of the deputy would likely alter his intentions and prevent further trouble.

Ed Gault, however, had other ideas. Learning of the escape the next morning, he mounted his horse and struck out for Shibolem, determined to track down the three men and jail them as a precaution against any further problems.

The lawman returned the succeeding day with the word that he had been unable to locate Weber and his friends. It was his guess they had moved on, probably to another town. Slater was skeptical but as the days passed and they saw no more of the trio, he began to accept the belief.

Matters were going much smoother now where the crew was concerned. Their hostility had disappeared and all were willing workers, seemingly as anxious and de-

termined as he to complete the drive successfully. Ed
Gault continued to ride with them much of the time,
periodically doubling back to the settlement to check on
his office and handle routine matters, then catching up
to the slow-moving herd the following day.

Slater kept well to the east side of the vast plain, placing as much ground as possible between the drive and
the ragged butte area in the west where the outlaws were
said to hang out. That the movement of the herd was still
unnoticed Dow knew was an impossibility; they had
gradually worked out of the lush grassland, were now
angling across an expanse studded with snakeweed, cactus, and rabbitbush. Forage was poor, and while the cattle did not suffer, a large pall of yellow dust now hung
above the herd that was visible for miles.

Adding to the tension that had begun to build inside
Slater was the failure of the deputy to return after his
latest departure for Shibolem. Always before it had been
his habit to ride out early one morning, put in an appearance late the next; there had been no sign of him now,
however, for two days.

"Just when we're liable to be needing him the most,"
John Ledge commented that evening when they halted
for camp, "he ain't nowheres around."

The following day a heavy shower fell which was of
some help, soothing the steers as well as laying the dust
to some extent, but it made for a fireless camp since there
was no dry wood available and the supply they had
brought along from the ranch was exhausted.

"As soon we'd show no smoke, anyway," Slater said
to the men as they all stood near the pack horses making

a meal of hard biscuits, dried beef, and pickled peaches. Each man still wore his ankle-length yellow slicker, and grouped there in the murky light they looked strange, unreal. "If we've been spotted by the outlaws it'll be to-night or in the morning they'll hit us."

"Can't be but a day or two out of McCoy, can we?" Farley said, staring off into the south.

"From what I was told about the country, we ought to be getting there late tomorrow or maybe the next morning."

"About right," Kargill said, and pointed to a long, low finger of land rising up from the plain. "That there's Hupperman Ridge. It sort of divides things. We keep to the left of it for McCoy. Them rustlers, after they made their raids, drove the cattle they got away with down the right-hand side and straight into Mexico."

"And near as I recollect," Ledge added, "it was always somewheres along here that them jaspers pulled the raids."

"From about here on 'til we get to the point of the Ridge," Kargill agreed.

Slater nodded, said: "Well, if we can keep clear of them until around noon tomorrow, we'll have it licked."

Ledge, washing down the meal with a swallow of water from his canteen, frowned. "How so?"

"Haven't mentioned it to you but we've got some help waiting for us if we need it, once we get fairly close to McCoy—the Army."

"Army?" Kargill echoed. "Since when'd they move in?"

"Not exactly sure but they're there now. The colonel's

a friend of Mrs. Darrow and Glenna made some arrangements with him—on the quiet."

"Dang that little gal!" Ledge said, grinning. "She's sure one to write home about! I savvy now why she was so all fired sot on making this drive."

Aaron Kargill wagged his head. "She's a pistol, all right," he agreed, and looked wistfully off toward the Ridge. "Only wish't we was a mite closer."

Slater agreed silently but there was no possibility of such. Had the cattle not been tired and if the night was going to be one filled with bright moonlight instead of heavily overcast, they might have been able to push the herd on until they reached the towering landmark and were in an area where they could expect to encounter troopers. But it was out of the question.

"The Army camping at McCoy?" Ledge wanted to know.

"Some place close by. Glenna didn't know exactly where. Big thing for us to remember is if we do get raided tomorrow, or even tonight, try to keep the herd running for the east side of the Ridge. If we're lucky the soldiers will hear the shooting and come give us a hand."

"Yeh, if they ain't at McCoy," Farley muttered. "It's still a far piece to there and they ain't likely to hear no gunshots if that's where they are."

Aaron Kargill clawed at his beard, looked off into the black night toward the bluffs. "Expect we won't be long in finding out," he said, and then came back to face Slater. "Just aiming to mention it—I've got a rifle in my saddleboot you're mighty welcome to."

A stillness fell across the big man's features. He was silent for a long breath, and shrugging turned to his horse. "Obliged just the same . . . Let's get scattered. Herd's going to need watching over closer than ever tonight."

"Yeh," John Ledge agreed, and added sourly, "I'd even welcome seeing Royce Darrow riding in right now—and that danged deputy."

"You sure ain't hard to please," Kargill replied, climbing stiffly onto his saddle, "but I reckon them's my sentiments, too . . . See you all later."

The sky cleared during the early morning hours and with the first brightening in the east, they got the cattle into motion, foregoing even a simple breakfast. The long, irregular shape of Hupperman Ridge, cold and barren-looking in the early light, stood before them in the distance like a dark barrier, and Slater riding just ahead of the old steer captaining the herd, led the long-horned beast toward its forward point.

The land had changed, had become broken and rocky, and progress was much slower. The cattle fought continually to veer right and stay on smoother ground where there was more grass in evidence. Slater hailed in Ledge who was riding the east flank at the time, sent him to assist Farley on the opposite, troubled side. Kargill, at drag and burdened with the extra horses as well as the pair packing supplies, did what he could to help while still keeping after the laggards and strays.

It was hard work and a steady struggle but finally they were just off the point and the cattle at last began to swing toward the long, narrow valley lying to the east of the ridge.

"Reckon we've done it!" Farley yelled to Slater as he galloped by in pursuit of a steer determined to take off on a course of his own. "They're heading right for McCoy!"

Dow waved his acknowledgment, wheeled to fall back and join Kargill, see if all was well with him. A sudden flurry of gunshots sounded, the reports muffled and remote above the noise of the moving cattle. Slater drew up short. Raising himself in his stirrups, he threw his glance about, trying to locate the source of the shots.

He saw the raiders a moment later—vague figures in the haze rushing toward them from the welter of rocks and brush at the end of Hupperman Ridge.

"It's them!" he heard Tom Farley shout from off to his right. "They been laying there—waiting for us!"

The cattle were beginning to slow, shifting uncertainly as the outlaws, shooting as they came, bore directly for them. If they could bring the herd to a halt, start it to milling, they would have little trouble swinging the steers to the west side of the ridge. Dow brought his nervously dancing horse about, hearing the pound of hoofs. It was Kargill and Ledge. Guns drawn, they were racing to meet the outlaws.

"Forget them!" Slater yelled, jerking his slicker loose from the strings that held it loosely to his saddle. "Stay after the cattle—stampede them!"

At once the two cowhands swerved in behind the lagging steers. Farley loomed up then through the thin dust, joined them, and yanking out his pistol, added his firing to theirs. Slater, crowding in beside them, began to swing the slicker wildly overhead, slapping at the rumps of the steers with the crackling yellow garment and yelling loudly.

The cattle seemed to hesitate, and then as if released by some unseen trigger, they veered hard left, began to flow down the slight grade that lay before them. The outlaws, barely visible through the thickening haze, continued their approach, but the herd, pushed hard by Slater and the crew, were cutting away from them and shortly the thundering mass of brown, black, and white bodies was pouring into the valley east of the ridge.

"Keep after them!" Dow shouted, roweling his horse and sending him plunging ahead.

Kargill and Ledge, their features strained; reddened, knotty fingers fumbling a bit as they reloaded their weapons, kept pace with him. Farther over he could see Farley, pistol pointed skyward, firing while he crowded the rumps of the steers in front of him.

On beyond the old puncher Dow could see the outlaws. Caught between the end of the rocky formation and the right flank of the herd, they were pulling to a stop, uncertain as to what they could do to turn the racing cattle.

And then, as if to settle the question they had in mind, a bugle sounded from somewhere close by in the valley, the notes high and clear above the pounding hoofs.

Slater eased back on his saddle, a tight grin on his lips as he slowed his horse. They'd hit it lucky. The Army, or a part of it, had been near, and the cavalrymen were rushing up to investigate the gunshots. He swung his attention toward the point of the ridge. The outlaws had wheeled, were galloping for the buttes in the distance.

14

McCoy was a railroad spur, a dozen weathered shacks, a sprawl of cattle pens and a large general store with a saloon in the back that offered rooms on a second floor to anyone finding it desirable or necessary to remain overnight.

Leaving the herd with the crew at a watering pond west of the corrals, Slater rode in and halted at the rack fronting the rambling building. He was winding the leathers around the tie bar when a paunchy, red-faced man came out onto the porch, and, hands thrust into the pockets of his shiny serge pants, confronted him.

"I'm Reece Tallman. You bring in that herd I seen down there?"

Slater nodded. "From the Darrow ranch. Supposed to meet a buyer here, name of Lewis. He around?"

"Darrow, eh? Was a young fellow putting up here for a spell claimed that was his name. He some kin?"

"Son . . . You said was—he pull out?"

"Sure did. Yesterday."

Dow gave that thought. He had expected Royce to be there waiting, and ready to accompany him and the crew on the return trip. Darrow apparently had other plans.

"What about Lewis?"

"Inside. You got a hand-shake deal with him?"

"Maybe. Why?"

Tallman's thick shoulders stirred. "I'm in the cattle buying business myself—along with owning this place," he said. "You don't get your price from Lewis, I'll be obliged if you'll give me a chance at your herd."

"Sure. Where'll I find Lewis?"

"Like I said, inside. Come on in, belly up to the bar and have yourself a drink. I'll roust him out for you."

Dow stepped up onto the wide porch, followed the man into the building. The saloon occupied the area beyond the store proper which was somewhat sparsely stocked with groceries, clothing, miscellaneous gear that trail hands might find need for. Moving through the rough built counters, Slater entered the shadowy saloon, paused just inside the connecting door to let his eyes adjust to change.

"Bar's over there," Tallman said, pointing to the opposite side of the room. "Just help yourself—we can square up later . . . I'll get Lewis."

Dow watched the man turn to a narrow stairway and start the climb for a balcony-like second level. He waited until the storekeeper had reached the top of the steps, and moved then to the short counter. Two men and a woman were at its far end and as he reached for one of several glasses set in a tray, and took up a partly filled bottle of whiskey standing nearby, he felt their glance upon him.

Pouring himself a drink, Slater turned slowly, hooked his elbows on the edge of the pegged slab, and surveyed the saloon's interior. The two cowhands and the woman were no longer watching him, he saw as he took in the area. There were a half a dozen tables with chairs in the rear, and he guessed there were times when Tallman's place was crowded.

Royce Darrow . . . His thoughts swung to the man. Tallman said he had been there, had ridden out only that day before. Slater swore under his breath, and tossing off the drink, helped himself to another. As well forget Royce; irresponsible and undependable, it would be senseless to plan on his presence for the return trip to Shibolem and the ranch. Just as he had shirked his duty on the drive, he would do so again . . . But if Deputy Ed Gault failed to show up, that would mean he would have only three guns siding him when he headed back with the money he would receive for the herd . . . But he'd not worry about it yet. The lawman surely would put in his appearance—and who could tell, Royce Darrow might also.

A door slammed somewhere on the upper floor and immediately the heavy tread of Tallman sounded as he walked the length of the gallery and began to descend the stairs. He had scarcely reached the bottom when the door slammed again.

Looking up Dow saw a small, sharp-faced man clad in a checked suit and wearing a narrow brimmed hat step into view. Behind him, hands doing something to her hair, came one of the saloon women. He'd interrupted something, Slater guessed.

The buyer descended the stair, crossed to him, hand outstretched. "I'm Jeb Lewis," he said genially. "Tallman tells me you're the drover from the Darrows."

Slater said, "I am. We're holding the herd at the pond."

"Good. Been expecting you for a week or more, was about to give you up. Nobody ever trails into here from the north—"

"Didn't Royce Darrow tell you we were on the way?" Dow cut in, frowning. "Understand he's been here for several days."

Lewis stroked his chin, looked puzzled. "Sure wasn't anybody by that name talked to me. Was he supposed to?"

"Kind of expected he would—"

"Well, was several men hanging around here, some of them laying over from a drive that came up from the south, others that don't seem to have nothing special to do. Guess he was here all right if you say so but I sure didn't meet with him. It make a difference—him not being here, I mean?"

There was no understanding Royce Darrow, Slater thought, and shook his head. "No, it's all the same."

"Fine. Guess we can get on with it . . . What'd you say your name was?"

Dow had not mentioned it but he said, "Slater . . . The price you quoted the Darrows still hold?"

"Still does—twenty dollars a head for good beef."

Slater glanced beyond the man to Tallman, question in his eyes. A few dollars more would be a big help to Glenna in her plan to rebuild the Circle D. But the store-keeper shook his head.

"Expect we can start tallying then," Dow said, swinging his attention back to Lewis. "You ready now?"

"Any time you say. How many did you bring in?"

"Started with four hundred head. Lost three or four, maybe a half dozen," Dow replied, laying a half dollar on the bar for his drinks.

"No trouble with outlaws?"

"Some. Army showed up just in time to drive them off."

"Ah, yes—the Army," Lewis said as they moved toward the door. "I'm trying hard to get them to establish a permanent post here at McCoy. Wrote Washington a hat full of letters about it but all I get is promises to look into it . . . You go on, bring up your cattle. I'll meet you at the pen—the one at this end."

The final count made after the steers were driven through a chute and into a high-fenced enclosure came out four steers short of the original four hundred head. It was small loss, Slater guessed, considering the attempted raid on the herd, for if luck, in the shape of a nearby cavalry patrol, had not been with them when the outlaws struck, the figure could have been much larger.

"Sure is a mighty good feeling," John Ledge said as they walked their horses toward Tallman's. "This here's just like the old days when John Darrow was alive and kicking. I aim to buy myself a quart of liquor and do me some real celebrating tonight." He paused, leaned forward on his saddle and stared intently at Slater. "We are staying over 'til morning, ain't we, boss?"

They were strung out abreast, riding side by side. Lewis had gone on ahead when the final tally was made, telling Dow that he would meet him in the saloon and settle up.

"I figure we're due a little celebrating—and a good night's sleep," he replied. "We'll rent a couple of Tallman's rooms, layover until morning. Gault ought to be here by then."

"Been meaning to ask," Kargill said, "where's Royce? Figured he'd at least be out there at the loading chute."

"Was here several days, then rode off yesterday, so I'm told."

There was a moment's silence, and then Farley said: "Sure beats all! Lays around here waiting for us and then when we show up, he takes out. That boy'll do anything to get out of work."

"Well, I ain't caring nothing about him," John Ledge said, with a wave of his hand. "What I'm wanting to know is this Tallman got any women around the place?"

Kargill hooted. "Women! Why dang it, you can't do no woman any good!"

"I sure'n hell can try, and feeling the way I do right now—right peart and plenty proud over what we've gone and done—I just might cut the mustard!"

"By jeebies, if you can, so can I!" Kargill declared. "You game, Tom?"

"Ain't never backed away from a good-looking woman yet," Farley said. "Might take a bottle or two of booze, but I'm with you."

Dow Slater smiled. This was a different crew from the one that had begun the drive. They seemed to have shed the years along with the attitude of apathy and defeat he had noted at their first meeting. A new outlook had taken over, filling them with a measure of pride and giving them the feeling they were working cowhands again, and riding for a ranch that was a going concern.

They reached Tallman's, halted at the hitchrack, and then on second thought, Slater led the way around to the rear where he had noted a corral and a barn. A hostler came forth to meet them, and, turning their horses over to him, they doubled back for the main building. Abruptly Slater checked his stride, turned to the stableman.

"About forgot. We left our pack horses and remuda back in one of the loading pens. Be obliged if you'll look after them too—hay and a little grain."

The hostler nodded and they continued on, the men hurrying a bit in their anxiety to get inside the saloon and partake of its hospitality.

The rear door of the place swung open. The men Slater had seen at the bar stepped out, descended the half a dozen steps leading down from the landing, and walked quickly toward the corral where two horses waited.

John Ledge slowed his steps, eyes follwing them while a frown twisted his leathery face. Dow glanced back at him.

"Somebody you know?"

The old puncher rubbed at the back of his neck, hastened to catch up. "That there little short jasper, one wearing a red shirt—seems I've seen him before. Can't just recollect where."

"In Shibolem, maybe—"

"Could be . . . Aaron, them two that just come out, you get a gander at them?"

"Never paid them no mind. Why?"

"One with a red shirt—got a feeling we've met somewheres."

Kargill, climbing the steps with surprising agility, cast a glance over his shoulder at the pair. They had mounted, were pulling away from the corral. He shook his head.

"Don't look familiar to me. Gone now, anyways," he added, jerking open the door. "Mister Bartender, here we come! Set us out your best drinking liquor and trot out your pretty gals—we're aiming to paint this here town red!"

Slater stepped aside, allowed the men to crowd by, cross to the bar. Tallman was now behind it, and there were four women sitting at a table just beyond. They viewed the elderly cowhands with no enthusiasm.

Glancing about Slater located Lewis in a far corner and moved toward him, hesitating briefly at the counter.

"We'll be needing a couple of rooms for the night," he said to Tallman, and then ducked his head at the crew, setting up a clamor at the opposite end of the bar. "Give them whatever they want and put it on my tab. I'll settle with you before we pull out."

The saloonman nodded and Dow continued on to where the buyer, several papers, a book of some sort and a cash box before him, was awaiting. Placing his back to the others in the room, Slater sat down.

"Bill of sale's all ready and I've got a receipt for you to sign," Lewis said. "Put the Darrows' name, by you, on them and the money's all yours—seven thousand nine hundred and twenty dollars."

Dow took the pencil from him, affixing the necessary signatures. "As soon it wasn't cash," he said.

"That's what the Darrows asked for—cold cash. Didn't want a draft. Some reason for it, I guess."

"A good one," Slater replied, settling back to watch the man count out the money. He went no further into the matter; Glenna's reason was personal and he saw no cause to reveal the straits in which the girl had found herself and that had brought about the unusual request.

Lewis laid out the amount before him, most of it in currency, some of it in gold double eagles. Dow Slater gathered it in, thrust the paper bills inside his shirt, dropped the coins into a side pocket. He'd buy a money belt from Tallman; that would be the safest way to carry it—strapped around his middle and out of sight. There was small likelihood of trouble anyway since no one, other than Lewis, would know he'd have the cash on him. Besides he'd have the crew as well as Deputy Ed Gault siding him.

Rising, he shook hands with Lewis, promising to relay his appreciation to the Darrows and express the hope of doing business the next year, and returned to the bar. There he took a place alongside Ledge and the others who had succeeded in interesting two of the women in having a drink with them. Beckoning, he called Tallman aside.

"You got a safe I can use for the night?" he asked quietly.

The storekeeper nodded. "Sure have. Got a A-number one dandy. Had to get it. Cattle buyers coming here and wanting to keep their money and papers in a safe place forced me to buy one . . . Just follow me."

Slater trailed the man into the store part of the building, halted before a small, iron door in a wall. Twisting the combination knob, Tallman swung back the thick panel, pointed to one of a half a dozen numbered metal cash boxes, all with padlocks.

"Take your pick," he said, "then stick the key in your pocket. I'll do the rest."

Slater complied with the instructions and stepped back, watched the man close the door and spin the knob.

"Be yours when you're ready for it," Tallman said, facing him. "Ain't never lost a nickel."

Dow nodded in satisfaction. The money was safe and he could forget it—at least until morning. Meanwhile he'd enjoy himself, take it easy.

Retracing his steps to the saloon, he halted inside the door, a stir of loneliness moving through him. It would be nice if Judith were somewhere nearby and he could go see her—be with her. It was a new and strange feeling to Dow Slater. Never before had there been anyone he cared enough about to note their absence, and he guessed that had a deep meaning . . . He just might take that job Glenna had offered him as foreman of the Circle D—then he'd be in a position to see Judith as often as he wished.

15

They were late in rising and Slater, the first downstairs, took his breakfast of steak, eggs, and coffee alone at a table near the bar. When he had finished he went into the store section of the building where Tallman sat in a chair tipped against a wall reading a yellowed newspaper, and claimed the money stored in the safe for him.

Choosing a money belt from the merchant's small stock, he stepped back into a corner, out of sight, and transferred the currency and gold coins, except for two double eagles, into the pockets of the canvas and leather strap and buckled it around his waist, inside his shirt.

"Reckon you're in the market for a gun, too," Tallman said when Dow came back into the center of the room. "Man toting that much cash around ought to have a side arm."

Slater shook his head. "Got three good men riding with me, and I'm looking for a deputy to show up. I'll have plenty of protection . . . How much I owe you?"

Tallman stared off through the open doorway. The steel tracks of the railroad curving past his building on their way to the loading pens glistened brightly in the sunlight.

"Let's see," he began thoughtfully, "was the two rooms,

the meals, the whiskey and the tequila—quite a bit of both, that belt, keep for your animals and a night's rent on the safe . . . Let's make it thirty dollars. Fair enough?"

Slater handed over the two twenty-dollar coins he'd held out, pocketed the change.

"You pulling out soon?" Tallman asked.

"Right away. When you see my crew tell them I'm down at the barn getting the horses ready."

"Sure thing . . . Obliged to you for your business."

Dow crossed to the building's front entrance, stepped out onto the landing, and circling, made his way to the stable. The hostler was busy forking down hay from the half loft.

"Be there in a minute," he called.

"It's all right," Slater replied. "I can saddle my own horse."

The stableman resumed his work and Dow, locating the sorrel, began to throw on his gear. Finished, he moved to the next stall, began to get ready the bay that Tom Farley was riding. Halfway through the chore he heard boot heels on the hardpack outside, and glanced over the partition to the wide doorway. The sudden hope that Ed Gault had arrived, died. It was Ledge and the others.

They filed into the stable, silent, morose men all played-out from a night's activities their age found no longer possible to accept, and sought out their mounts. Farley, discovering his horse nearly ready, mumbled a spiritless thanks to Dow and fell to completing the task.

Returning to the sorrel, Slater backed the big gelding into the runway and led him out into the warming sunshine. The hostler was nowhere to be seen, likely was now with Tallman making sure that accounts had been squared.

"Slater!"

At the shout, Dow looked around. Ed Gault was coming from the side of the saloon. The lawman was smiling broadly.

"Been looking for you—was told I'd find you back here. Glad to see you made it through."

Dow took the deputy's proffered hand. "Was beginning to worry about you a little."

"Yeh, got tied up. You have any trouble?"

"Some. The Army stepped in, helped us out. Nobody got hurt."

"Glad to hear it. Didn't know they'd set up a post here. Surprised me when I seen the camp."

Farley and Ledge, leading their horses, came from the barn into the yard, bucked their heads glumly at the deputy. A moment later Kargill, already on the saddle of his buckskin, appeared.

"About time you showed up," he said, glaring at the lawman, and then added, "Come on, let's get cracking."

Slater made a gesture toward the cattle pens. "Go ahead, pick up the pack horses and the others. We'll catch up." He'd almost forgotten their supply of trail grub was running low on a few items—coffee, soda crackers, bacon, canned tomatoes, to mention those called to his attention by Kargill.

"Where's Royce?"

At Gault's question Slater shrugged. "Who the hell

knows? Was here, then rode out the day before we came in. Haven't seen him since that night he left camp."

The deputy swore deeply. "It just ain't in him to straighten up, seems . . . You ready to leave?"

"Soon as I do a little buying at the store," Dow said and swung onto the sorrel. "How about you?"

"Had figured on resting up for an hour or two, but there's no need. A couple of stiff drinks'll do me just as well. Go on do your buying, I'll meet you at the cattle pens."

An hour later they were on the way, riding abreast, the pack animals and the spare horses trailing behind. Kargill was slumped in his saddle, chin sunk into his chest as he slept. Ledge and Farley were having similar problems, both cheerless and struggling to stay awake. Dow, with Gault to his left, maintained silence, finding nothing to talk with the lawman about.

Around noon they drew abreast of the Army camp, which was pitched on a slope a mile or so to the east of the trail. The deputy reined in his horse.

"Going to leave you here for a bit," he said as Slater turned questioningly to him. "Want to do some talking to the commanding officer of the outfit."

Ledge grinned sleepily at the lawman. "You aiming to join the cavalry, Deputy?"

"Nope, looking for a jasper that busted jail over in San Antone. Been tipped off he signed up with the Army somewhere in this part of the country, figuring it a good way to hide out."

"We'll wait for you," Slater said, frowning.

"No sense in that. Got a Wanted dodger with his picture on it and it'll probably take me an hour or so to show it around. Slow as you're moving, I'll catch up easy."

Slater looked ahead. The crew with the remuda and pack horses had continued on, were drawing away.

"All right," he said in a reluctant voice, and spurred to overtake his party.

The day wore on. Around the middle of the afternoon they halted in a small coulee and there built a fire, made coffee and ate a little of their trail fare. Slater, moving to a small hillock, put his attention to the south. Two small dots in the far distance indicated riders; one could be the deputy, but there was no way of being sure. Gault should be returning, however. Dissatisfied, he walked slowly back to the camp, hearing the complaining voice of Aaron Kargill.

"I'll sure be real pleasured when dark comes and we can get some sleep . . . I ain't never been this beat."

"Me neither," Ledge muttered. "Hell, they plant folks in the graveyard that feel better'n me."

"You'll live through it," Slater snapped humorlessly. "Let's move out."

They pressed on, riding now along the east side of Hupperman Ridge which lay, like a rocky hogback, to their left. The area where the raiders had endeavored to hijack the herd was not far ahead. Kargill, brushing at bloodshot eyes with the back of a hand, glanced over his shoulder.

"Where you reckon that deputy is?"

Slater shrugged angrily. "Ought've caught us by now.

If he hasn't shown up by the time we reach the point, we'll pull in and wait."

"That'll be a right smart idea," Farley said, and then stiffened on his saddle. "Ain't that dust I'm seeing?"

Dow followed the man's leveled finger as they all came to a halt. A thin, tan haze was hanging low in the sky beyond the end of the ridge.

"Something there, all right," Ledge said. "Could be that bunch that jumped us."

"What do they want now?" Farley wondered. "We ain't got no steers for them to rustle."

"We got something better," Kargill said, "that there bank draft Slater's carrying."

Farley swore, dropped a hand to his pistol. "I reckon they could go somewheres and get it cashed, was they to know the right folks."

"Wonder which ones of them jaspers we seen hanging around Tallman's it is? Only recollect three, maybe four."

"It's somebody that's sure been keeping an eye on us."

Slater took no part in the conversation, not even to the extent of advising the men that there was no draft but cash money. His gaze was on the end of the ridge where it broke off and sloped down to meet the plain, and his attention was wholly centered there. The dust boil had faded, was no longer definite; but that could mean the source, rather than passing on down the opposite side of the formation, had halted—and was waiting for them.

"That pile of rocks over there," he said, pointing off to a ragged mound a quarter mile to their right, "we'll make for it and wait for Gault. Be a good place to make a stand if—"

"Too dang late for that now!" Ledge yelled suddenly as a half a dozen riders broke from the end of the ridge and raced toward them.

16

They'd never make it to the rocky mound. The riders, unquestionably outlaws and likely the same party that had made the attempt on the herd, would cut them off before they could reach it.

Taut, Slater put his attention on the country due east. A long mile ahead he could see a band of thin brush, and beyond that a few squat trees. It could mean an arroyo.

"This way!" he shouted, and jammed his spurs into the sorrel's flanks.

At once the others swept in beside him and in a ragged line, they pounded for the distant growth. Behind them the raiders opened up, their pistols making a hollow, popping sound above the thudding of the horses' hoofs.

Dow looked back. A tightness gripped him. They were losing ground. The outlaws, on comparatively fresh mounts, were narrowing the gap. Abruptly, on his left, Tom Farley began returning the raider's fire, twisting half about, holding his arm stiff as he triggered his heavy weapon. Immediately Kargill and John Ledge took their cue from him, added their efforts. But the advantage was all with the outlaws; leaning forward, steadying themselves on their horses by standing partly upright in the stirrups, they had better control of their guns.

Slater shifted his eyes on to the south, hope stirring through him. They were too far above the Army encampment for the shooting to be heard—but there were those two riders they had noticed, and there might be a patrol somewhere on the flats or in the short hills; one such as that which had intervened the day before when the herd was attacked . . . The country lay hot and empty under the sun.

Gault . . . Royce Darrow . . . Slater cursed them both bitterly as he crouched low over the straining sorrel while bullets thunked into the sand around them sending up spurts of dust or sang off rocks. Royce he could dismiss without thought, a useless, undependable wastrel. But the deputy; for all his evident promises to Glenna Darrow he had proved to be of no help at all on the drive.

And there was something wrong somewhere—Dow couldn't rid himself of the feeling. The failure of Gault to be around when needed, his lack of interest where Glenna's needs were concerned—and there was that matter of Tip Weber and his friends. Did the lawman have a hand in their escape? The thought had occurred to him before, now it was becoming a conviction.

Gault would have had the opportunity, and feigning sleep would be easy—but why would he do it? Judith's words came to him then, her remark that Ed Gault wanted the girl to fail so that his own interests might best be served, and Weber and the pair with him could have been part of a plan to halt the drive.

If true, and since that attempt failed, was it not logical to assume that the deputy had something to do with the raid on the herd—and now the ambush that had been waiting for them at the end of Hupperman Ridge? Again Dow Slater swore, savagely, deeply . . . It was all there, plain as it could be. He should have figured . . .

A bullet struck the horn of his saddle, screamed off into space. He threw a glance over his shoulder. The outlaws were closing in fast—the nearest, a man with a red shirt, only yards away. He looked vaguely familiar, and a moment later Dow remembered; one of the pair that had come out of Tallman's saloon when they first arrived. Ledge had thought he knew him, probably had noticed him as a member of the gang trying to hijack the cattle.

The hammer of guns was now a steady racket. Ed Gault was going to have it all his way, he thought, looking ahead. The brush and trees were still in the distance. It was an arroyo, he saw, evidently a fairly deep one.

"We get to that brush—scatter!" he yelled at the crew.

Kargill, hunched low, intent now on riding rather than shooting, bobbed his head. His features appeared lean, the skin stretched tight over the bones of his face. On beyond him Ledge and Tom Farley were continuing to use their pistols. Abruptly Farley sagged. The weapon fell from his grasp as he caught at the saddle horn to keep from falling.

A slash of fire ripped across Slater's ribs just below his left shoulder. He recoiled involuntarily, heard a shout and saw Aaron Kargill throw up his arms, begin to sway on the back of his buckskin. And then suddenly the arroyo was before him.

The sorrel soared out into thin air, came down solidly,

went to his knees. In an instant he had recovered, was up and racing for the band of stunted cedars a dozen yards farther on.

From the tail of his eye Slater could see Ledge. The puncher was bent low, had twisted about, allowing the reins to hang while he crooked his left arm and used it as a brace for his pistol. He saw nothing of Kargill or Farley, assumed both had gone down.

With Ledge only a length behind, Slater reached the cedars, swung the heaving sorrel hard left. The wash was wide, but a short distance on it narrowed and the brush rimming its high banks was thicker. If they could reach that, they might have a chance.

The sorrel began to slow, the loose footing taking quick toll of his ebbing strength. Ledge, too, was having difficulty with his black.

"We got 'em!"

The shout came from the edge of the arroyo above. Bullets slammed into the wall beyond Slater, lifted dirt around the sorrel's frantically digging hoofs, clipped through the dry branches of brush. He glanced up, saw the line of riders rushing toward him. Surprise rocked Dow Slater. One, near center, a big man with a flat crowned, plainsman's hat decorated with a brass studded band, was grinning down at him. Pete Reegan!

"Watch your shooting!" the outlaw yelled. "That'n on the sorrel—he's mine!"

In that next fragment of time Slater felt the gelding wilt, start to fall. From somewhere close by John Ledge cursed, and then as shocking pain roared through him he plunged into blackness.

17

Slowly, Dow Slater opened his eyes. All things were a hazy gray blur, but it was still daylight he knew because he could feel the sun bearing down upon him relentlessly. Motionless, he allowed his senses to clear. The left side of his face and neck were stiff with some sort of crust and the bee sting along his rib cage was now a dull burn. His entire, sweat steeped body was a length of aches and his head throbbed with sullen fury.

Gradually his vision returned and with it came a total awareness. He lay on the floor of the arroyo where he had been pitched when the sorrel died under him. A bullet must have hit him, too, at almost the same instant, grazed him, knocked him cold.

Shifting his eyes, he looked about. He was alone in the sandy wash—alone except for the bodies of John Ledge and Tom Farley, and the horses. Gently, he turned over, ignoring the pain that went screaming through him, and sat up.

Raising a hand he touched the stiffness on his face and neck. He had bled plenty from a groove an outlaw's bullet had carved along his head, just above an ear. But it was hardly more than that. There was a slight wound in one forearm of which he had not been conscious, and it, as with the place on his side, while also bleeding copiously, he considered unworthy of notice. In the past he had been wounded far worse several times.

Uncomfortable, but nothing serious; he suspected the wallop he'd taken when the sorrel threw him had done much greater damage than the bullet that had grazed his head and the two that had nicked his skin. Fortunately the depth of his unconsciousness and the generous amount of gore flowing from his body had convinced the outlaws that he was not alive, and they had left him at that.

Abruptly he looked down. His shirt had been jerked open and the money belt taken from around his waist. That was what they'd been after, of course—Glenna Darrow's money. Failing to rustle the herd, the outlaws, led by Pete Reegan, he recalled suddenly, had laid an ambush for him and the Circle D cowhands. Reegan had been aware of their every move—and to do that he would have had to have help outside his gang.

Fully conscious now, and burning with anger, Slater drew himself upright. The effort cost him a surge of sickening pain and he hung there stiffly for a long minute allowing it to pass, then moving slowly he walked to where Ledge lay. The old cowhand had died instantly, a bullet through the heart. Wheeling about, he crossed to Tom Farley. Death had come quickly to him also. Kargill would be back up on the flat, and laboriously climbing up out of the arroyo, Slater walked the short distance to where the man, a dusty, crumpled heap of clothing, had fallen.

He had known Aaron would not be alive but it had

been necessary to be certain. Hunched beside the older man, he studied the set, bearded face for several minutes, rose finally and made his way back into the sandy wash. His head was swimming, and going to the side of the sorrel he removed the canteen from his saddle, pulled the cork and poured a quantity of its contents over his head. He felt better at once. Cupping a hand, he filled it with the water, applied it to the wound above his ear, relieving some of the crustiness that surrounded it and extended down his face and neck. Considerably improved, Slater took a swallow of the tepid liquid, replaced the cork, and brushing at the sweat misting his eyes, again drew himself upright.

A deep, pulsing fury had replaced the shock and anger that had come with first consciousness. And now it grew stronger as he relived in his mind those last few minutes —the wild flight across the flat, Kargill throwing his arms wide when a bullet drove into him; that fraction of suspended time when the sorrel paused at the edge of the arroyo, hunched his big body to leap, and then the solid jolt as his hoofs hit the sand.

Farley clinging to his saddle horn, the oath blurting from John Ledge's mouth when he was hit; Pete Reegan's voice rising above the confusion, *Watch your shooting! The one on the sorrel—he's mine!*

Reegan . . . He'd known they'd meet again one day. The outlaw had evidently pulled out, forsaken Kansas after Powderville, just as he had done. The law had probably made it much too hot for him and he had headed west looking for safer pastures. It was ironic that he had chosen the very area where the man responsible for his leaving Kansas had found fit to stop and begin a new life; or was it so strange? Could Pete Reegan have somehow known that he would be the man bossing the Darrow trail drive to McCoy? If so, then the outlaw had evened the score—or thought he had. Regardless, it didn't end there.

Slater, leaning back against the arroyo's wall to ease his aching body, considered what lay ahead for him; track down Reegan and his bunch, recover Glenna Darrow's money—and make them pay for the deaths of the three men they had killed. Once that was accomplished he would return to Shibolem and the Circle D and call to account Deputy Ed Gault . . . But first he must see to the bodies of the crew.

He had nothing with which to dig graves, and so, dragging the men to the side of the arroyo where there was an overhang, he caved the sandy clay in upon them until they were well covered. It was hard work and when it was finally done, he sank back weakly into the shade of a small cedar, heaving for breath and drenched with sweat. It came to him then that he was afoot.

The fact struck him with solid force, and getting to his feet he again climbed out of the wash and threw his glance out across the plain. Of the four horses, only Kargill's buckskin had not died in the arroyo. He was nowhere to be seen, probably had trailed off after the outlaws when they rode on, or possibly had been taken possession of by one of them. And there was no sign of the extra horses or the pack animals they had brought on the drive. When Reegan and his men had begun their attack, they had scattered, could be anywhere by that time.

Glancing at the lowering sun, Slater wheeled, stolidly returned to the floor of the arroyo. He was in a bad way, but it would make no difference; he wasn't giving up. The outlaws had killed three good men, robbed him, left him for dead and ridden on. That was Reegan's way; to him life meant nothing—only gold counted.

If he had been carrying a gun maybe matters would have worked out differently; maybe John Ledge and Aaron Kargill and Tom Farley would be alive and he wouldn't be trapped in a near hopeless situation. Anger soaring anew through him, Slater reached down, snatching up the pistol that had fallen from Ledge's hand.

Impatient, he brushed the grit from the weapon, tried its feel in his palm. The butt nestled perfectly, felt cool, comfortable . . . Goddam Pete Reegan and his bunch! He'd hunt them down—kill them—make them pay with their lives if it took . . .

Dow Slater's suddenly raging thoughts came to a full stop . . . Powderville . . . A room filled with acrid smoke . . . A woman's hopeless eyes—screams . . . The deafening blast of guns. And now three more dead crudely buried in the floor of an arroyo. With a savage oath Slater hurled the weapon off into the brush.

There had to be another way! He'd find Reegan and his gang, recover Glenna Darrow's money, all right—but he'd do it without a gun. He'd find that way, and in the end the outlaws would die—but it wouldn't be by a gun held in his hand . . . And far as his having had a gun to use during the attack, it would have made little, if any difference.

Taking up his canteen and saddlebags, he slung them over his shoulder and climbed out of the wash. The sun was almost gone and he stood motionless, silhouetted against the darkening sky while he mulled over his best course.

There was no wisdom in heading back for McCoy, and Shibolem, days to the north, was out of the question. Besides, there was no time to waste; it was important that he get on the trail of the outlaws. On foot it would be slow, and considering the condition he was in, most painful; but somewhere the trail would end. One important factor favored him; they thought him dead, they would not be expecting him.

Moving slow, he began to walk the edge of the arroyo. Shortly he found where Reegan and his crowd had approached. He followed the tracks down into the wash, noted where they had left their mounts during the few minutes they remained, and then picked up the hoof marks left when they climbed out on the opposite bank.

Six horses. They had struck off due east. There evidently was a town of some sort in that direction for which they headed. Grim, he began the pursuit.

18

Night closed swiftly. Slater seemed barely to notice, his eyes on the hoofprints of the outlaws' horses, moving side by side across the plain. Darkness brought no problem insofar as following them was concerned; the recent rain had raised a slight crust in the soil and the marks were easily visible, became even more so when the moon began to spread its light across the land.

But weariness caught up with him eventually, and around midnight, exhausted, he sank down onto the sand of shallow wash to rest, catch a few moments' sleep. He dropped off immediately intending to be up and again on the move shortly. But the built-in clock on which he had always relied failed him and it was the chill of pre-dawn that finally roused him, brought him angrily to his feet.

He moved off at once, the pearl glare of first light in his eyes. He'd lost hours and there was no way they could be recovered, he realized, blaming himself bitterly. It could mean the difference in overtaking Pete Reegan and his men, and missing them completely.

The sun came out, filling the sky with streaks of rose and purple, washing into a pale gold and then changing to a steel blue devoid of clouds. He began to feel the heat but he pressed on doggedly, never losing sight of the hoofprints. Late in the morning the throbbing of his head had become so intense he sought relief by binding his bandanna tightly about it, and a stiffness had developed in his left side.

Eventually he discarded the saddlebags, and by noon the contents of his canteen had shrunk to a half a dozen swallows. The heat continued to rise and sweat clothed his body, covering his face in glossy patches, but he did not alter his pace, slogged stoically on.

Unexpectedly the grumbling of a moving wagon reached him. Slater pulled up short, hope shooting through him, and then abruptly he broke into an erratic, unsteady run, dodging the clumps of snakeweed and rabbitbush and prickly pear cactus. A dozen yards and he halted again. Before him were the twins ruts of a fairly well-traveled road, and a distance up their curving course a team and wagon were coming into view, also heading east. He glanced then at the tracks of the outlaws' horses; they had swung onto the road.

Sucking for wind after the brief run, sweat pouring off him, but filled with relief and elation, he took up a position in the center of the ruts and awaited the arrival of the wagon.

The driver was an old man; bearded, dressed in worn, bib overalls, collarless shirt and a battered hat, he pulled to a stop, watched Slater walk up to him with suspicious eyes.

"What're you wanting?" he demanded.

The answer was obvious but Dow said, "Need a ride."

"Where's your horse?"

"Dead. Set me afoot. Be obliged for a lift."

The oldster considered Slater for a few moments. "Well, all right. Climb in," he said, finally relenting. "Where you headed?"

"Nearest town," Dow replied, pulling himself wearily onto the seat.

"That'll be Goshen."

"You going there?"

"Yeh, reckon I am. Where I haul my supplies from."

Slater, breathing more normally, took a swallow of water from the canteen, eased the burning in his throat. He started to replace the stopper, paused, offered the container to the driver.

The old man wagged his head, small eyes again filled with suspicion as he took in Slater more closely.

"You look mighty bunged up for a man that only got hisself throwed," he said as the team got underway.

"Horse went off a cutbank."

"Don't see no gun on you either."

Slater smiled, shrugged his shoulders. "This Goshen, it a fair-sized town?"

"Ain't big, ain't little. Anyways, it's the only one in this part of the country."

Goshen, undoubtedly, was the destination Reegan and his friends had in mind. "It got a lawman?"

The old driver stiffened slightly. "Town marshal, name of Burke . . . Now, if you're in some kind of trouble I'll ask you to get off right now. I ain't about to get myself mixed up in no—"

"Keep your shirt on. Law's not looking for me."

"Maybe it is and maybe it ain't," the oldster mumbled, slowing the team. "I plain ain't taking no chances."

Slater slipped a hand inside his shirt, grasped an imaginary, hidden weapon. "Keep driving, farmer, and everything'll work out fine for you," he said in a cold voice. "All I want's a ride into town."

"Sure, sure," the man said hurriedly, Adam's apple bobbing in his thin neck. "Be whatever you say . . . And my name ain't Farmer, it's Peters . . . Just don't want no trouble."

"You won't get any. Give you my word on that."

Peters slid him a doubting glance, but said no more. Slater, the pain in his head and the aches in his body multiplying with each bounce of the empty wagon, looked ahead.

"Goshen much farther?"

"Couple hours," Peters answered, eyes narrowing. "You in a powerful hurry?"

"Maybe—"

"You aiming to meet somebody there, or something?"

"Or something," Slater replied laconically, leaning forward. It felt better somehow to be in that position, elbows on knees, shoulders slack, head low.

Peters stirred. Dow looked up quickly into the oldster's weathered face, patted his shirt front suggestively.

"Don't get any ideas about pushing me off this seat. You won't get away with it."

"Weren't thinking of no such a-thing," Peters mumbled.

Slater slumped forward again . . . With a gun a man

could get just about anything he wanted, do almost whatever he wished since everyone either respected or feared the promise of death. The weak became the strong, the cowardly the brave, but in the end there would be no peace of mind for any of them.

"You come far?" Peters asked cautiously.

"Kansas—originally."

"Been around these parts coming onto ten year, myself. Got me a little place up Cedar Mountain way. It ain't much but I'm getting by—me and my old woman. Mind telling me what you're called?"

Slater stirred. There was the possibility that Peters, after arriving in Goshen, might mention his name within Reegan's hearing. He would take no chances.

"Dow—"

"Dow, eh? Once knew some folks over in west Texas by the name of Dow."

"No kin of mine," Slater said, reaching for the canteen and having another drink. The container was empty after but one swallow. Legs braced against the jolting of the wagons, he looked beyond the team. On to the east he could see a band of dark green.

"That the town?" he asked, pointing.

Peters nodded. "Them's the trees along the creek. Goshen's sort of setting in the middle of them."

"Railhead?"

"Nope, crossroads. If you're looking to get to the railroad it's a ways south. Can take the stage, unless you buy yourself another horse."

Slater was only trying to get the lay of the country

straight in his head. McCoy, he thought, was now due west—or it could be southwest, he wasn't sure.

"You ever hear of a place called Shibolem?"

Peters repeated the name as he stared vacantly off into the distance. "No, sir, can't say as I have. It supposed to be around here somewheres?"

"Not certain where it is," Dow answered and let it drop.

They lapsed into silence after that, Peters wrapped in whatever it could be that filled his mind, Slater thinking back to the arroyo, to the deaths of the three Circle D cowhands, the robbery—the reappearance of Pete Reegan in his life. Everything had gone right for the outlaw, but that was about to end.

"Reckon there's the town," Peters said a time later. "You wanting to get off some place special?"

Dow shook his head, eyes on the collection of shacks and buildings, no more than a dozen at most, that made up the settlement.

"No, let me off when we come to that first barn. I'll walk the rest of the way."

"Be no trouble taking you on—"

"Want to wash up at the creek," Dow said, finding one reason as good as another. It would be best he enter the town unnoticed. "As soon folks wouldn't see me in the shape I'm in . . . Obliged to you for the ride."

"Reckon you're welcome," Peters replied, and slanted for the indicated structure.

19

Cleaning himself up so that he would attract less attention really would be a good idea, Slater thought, as he moved toward the creek, and it just might relieve some of his aches and pains. So, seeking out a well-hidden bend in the stream where the water pooled, he stripped off and spent a time soaking and washing the grime and crusted blood from his body. He didn't have much luck with his shirt; the stains were still evident when he was finished but they did appear old.

There was little he could do about the wound on his head other than cleanse it and reapply the bandanna bandage. The long, shallow gash cut by the outlaw's bullet was extremely tender and he had to forego the idea of pulling low his hat to hide it from curious eyes. The places on his side and forearm were minor and he wasted no effort on them; if matters worked out right, he'd drop by the local doctor's office and get patched up before heading back to Shibolem.

Feeling considerably better after the brief respite in the cool water, Slater dropped back to the road, and, keeping to the trees and brush along its shoulder, made his way to the settlement.

Reaching the end of the street, he halted, had his look.

It was a stage stop; he realized that immediately when he saw the fairly large depot with its corral of spare horses at the rear. That was a break; likely he could get himself a mount there at low cost since they usually had animals they considered no longer fit for coach work and were willing to part with them for a small cost.

There was the usual general store, set off to itself, a row of houses, one large saloon called the Great Western behind which were a string of huts for the convenience of the saloon women and their customers, he supposed; a large livery stable, a few other business concerns, and the marshal's office which occupied one half of a building that also housed a saddlery and gunshop.

It was a busy town. There were a dozen or more persons moving along the dusty walks in the fading afternoon, half that number gathered in front of the depot awaiting the arrival of the next stagecoach. He recalled that Peters had said Goshen was a crossroads; likely the stage routes intersected there, also, which would account for the more than ordinary activity in so small and remote a settlement.

There was no sign of the outlaws' horses at any of the hitchracks. He had not expected to see them; they would have been there some eighteen hours or so and their mounts would have been stabled—if Goshen had been the destination of Reegan and his men.

He had simply assumed they would head for the town after seeing the hoofprints turn into the road and point eastward, had paid no more attention to them once he was in the wagon with Peters. If he had figured wrong he'd have but one course to follow—return to the road and search about until he picked up the tracks and start trailing them again. This time, however, he'd be in a much better condition, and by making a deal for a horse and gear, he'd not be afoot.

Slater hurriedly reached into his pockets, sighed quietly. The few dollars he had were still there. The outlaws had not bothered to strip him, had been content to take only the money belt he had been wearing. True, his capital was low, but he'd manage a deal, somehow.

But there was little gained now in speculation. He could quickly determine what he would be faced with and then decide what must be done, simply by having a look in the Great Western. If the outlaws were not there, he'd then check with the livery stable. At one place or the other he would find the answer.

Entering the street Slater crossed over and moved toward the saloon. At the far end of town a stagecoach whirled into view and rushed up to the depot and the persons expecting it. A few interested bystanders gravitated in that direction, curious as to who might be arriving or passing through, but on the whole the coach's arrival seemed to disrupt Goshen's tempo but little.

Reaching the Great Western, Slater halted, drew up against its front corner and leaned against the wall. There was no way he could think of to disguise himself and make it possible to enter and not be recognized by Reegan and his gang, if they were inside. He gave it a bit of thought and then, stepping up onto the wide porch, stationed himself at the building's entrance. Waiting until he was certain no one was approaching the batwings from the inside or out, Dow pivoted and, standing up close to the swinging panels, looked over their curved tops into the saloon.

It was a large place with a surprisingly ornate bar complete with back mirror, numerous shelves of glasses and rows of bottles—one much too elaborate for a town of Goshen's size. Likely the owner of the Great Western had been able to purchase it cheap somewhere and bring it in to add class to his establishment.

Reegan was there. A tightness gripped Slater when his drifting eyes settled on the outlaw and the five men who rode with him. Two small tables had been pushed together to form a large one, and the men were seated around it, a bottle of liquor before each. A half a dozen women were in their company, some lounging against the backs of chairs, a couple finding places on the laps of two of the outlaws, who were making the most of it.

The pair he and the crew had encountered at Tallman's, the rider with the red shirt and his squat partner, were part of the gang; Ledge had been right when he claimed to have seen them during the raid; it had been Pete Reegan all along—and he had known every move they made.

Winter cold, Slater studied the outlaws, carefully registering the features of each man in his mind. Elsewhere in the saloon business was brisk. A dozen patrons were at the long bar, several of the tables were occupied by card players, but it was the outlaw gang upon whom the women centered their attention; it was clear to them that there was where the money was to be had.

Dow considered his next move. It was important that he act soon and reclaim the stolen cash before too much of it was squandered. If he had a weapon it would be no problem; he could simply walk in, throw down on the outlaws, force them to give up under the threat of death.

But he had no gun, and there was that deep, strong current running through him that denied the use of such, outlaws or not. To pursue that course, one no stranger to him and employed many times before during his years as a lawman, would mean a shootout; men, possibly bystanders would die—and he had no stomach for that. There had to be another way. He'd told himself that several times, now assured himself once again.

The town marshal . . . Pulling back Slater stepped down into the street, crossed purposefully to the lawman's quarters. He'd lay it all out for the man, give him the details and swear out complaints against Pete Reegan and his crowd. Robbery and murder, they would be the charge. He could back his claims by taking the marshal—Burke, Peters had said his name was—to where he had buried the three members of the Circle D crew, bolster them further if necessary by referring him to Tallman and Lewis at McCoy.

He would suggest to the lawman that he swear in several special deputies. Reegan would not be taken easily. Dow knew that from experience. Handled right, bloodshed could be avoided.

Halting on the landing, he tried the door. It was

locked. Frowning, Slater shaded his eyes and peered through the window. There was no one inside.

"You looking for the marshal?"

At the question, Dow Slater came about, faced a squat, younger man wearing a pocketed apron over his clothing.

"I am—"

"Ain't around. Rode over to Lordsburg day before yesterday. Won't be back for at least a week."

20

Slater swore deeply. Pulling off his hat he ran long fingers agitatedly through his hair. The aproned man stared at the makeshift bandage, frowned.

"You needing help, mister? My name's Wingate. I run the shop next door and sort've look out for things when the marshal's gone . . . Maybe I can do something for you."

Dow nodded. "There's six outlaws over there in the saloon that held me up, robbed me of near eight thousand dollars. Killed three of my men doing it and rode off leaving me for dead, too. I want some help arresting them."

Wingate's eyes were filled with doubt. "Eight thousand dollars—that's a hell of a lot of money for—"

It was his appearance, Dow realized. No one would believe that he would be carrying such a large amount of cash, not judging from his looks.

"Name's Slater," he explained. "Drove a herd of cattle down from a town called Shibolem—somewhere north and west of here—to the railhead at McCoy. Money belongs to the people who owned the cows."

Wingate was shaking his head. "Can see the fix you're in, but I don't see how—"

"All I need is six or eight armed men to walk in there with me—"

"But without Burke they won't have no authority!"

"No problem getting around that. Can handle the whole thing as a citizen's arrest."

"What's that?"

"Where people step in and act for the law when there's no lawman handy," Slater said, eyes on the batwings of the Great Western. The outlaws could decide to split up, go their separate ways, and if that occurred his chances for recovering the money would be greatly diminished.

"I just don't know," Wingate said hesitantly. "If they're killers like you claim, I don't think I ought to get myself mixed up in it. Expect you'll find everybody else around here'll feel pretty much the same. Arresting hardcases like them's the marshal's business."

"Hell, I know that, but he's not around! Time he gets back they'll be gone."

The saddlemaker shrugged. "Reckon that's right but I don't see no help for it. Now, you can go ahead and talk to some of the other men if you're of a mind, but I'm plenty sure their answer'll be the same as mine."

Slater nodded resignedly. "Probably will. Lordsburg the nearest town where I can find a lawman?"

"Yeh, sure is—and it's two days hard riding . . . You lose your gun when they jumped you? Be glad to loan you whatever you want."

"Obliged, but I don't carry a weapon."

Wingate's eyes spread in disbelief. "You're looking for somebody to go in there after a half a dozen killers but you back off using a gun yourself? Mister, you must be loco! If you ain't ready to do a little fighting for yourself, you sure can't expect others to give you a hand!"

"Forget it," Slater snapped brusquely, and turned away.

Cutting back across the street, he halted in the deepening shadows of a passageway that lay between two buildings standing a short distance north of the saloon. Thinking it over, he reckoned it was too much to ask a plain citizen to face hardened outlaws such as Pete Reegan and his gang—particularly when he was refusing to use a weapon himself. But he had felt certain a good show of force would have had its effect on the killers.

That was all downstream now, however, and hashing it over gained nothing. He would have to come up with another plan—abruptly he drew back deeper into the shadows. The batwings of the Great Western had swung open. The outlaw wearing a red shirt and his squat companion, undoubtedly known as Shorty, had come out onto the porch with two of the women.

Each man had a bottle of whiskey by the neck, and with the women, one in a bright yellow dress, the other in discolored red, came off the landing, joking and laughing, and rounding the corner of the saloon, headed for the cribs behind it.

Immediately Dow Slater, a glimmer of an idea brightening in his mind, stepped out of the darkness, and gaining the narrow passage that lay alongside the Great Western, turned into it. The two couples were just ahead. Staying well back out of sight, Slater watched them approach the huts, Shorty and Redshirt staggering considerably. The latter, free hand gripped tightly by the girl in red, paused before the entrance to the second crib for a moment, and then followed her inside. Shorty, trailing along behind the woman in yellow, continued with her until they reached the fifth hut in the row. Halting long enough for the outlaw to take a lengthy pull at his bottle, she led him into the small structure.

Slater, mind working swiftly, and waiting until he was certain both doors were closed, proceeded quietly along the fronts of the shacks. This could be his opportunity, assuming all intended to satisfy their need for female companionship. Coming one or two at a time he could handle them; the one possibility of trouble would be if they all chose to visit the cribs with their lady friends at the same time.

It was worth gambling on—and like as not it was his only chance to recover Glenna Darrow's money before it was gone. Easing up to the second hut, he looked closely at the door. It was the usual makeshift slab affair held together with two crosspieces. A hasp and staple made it possible to keep it locked from the outside when the quarters were not in use, an ordinary thumb latch fastened it from the interior.

Crouched, he listened to the low mutter of voices. The woman laughed. The bottle clinked against something metal, and then there was silence. Slater took a deep breath, reached for the latch, throwing a glance toward the saloon. There was no one in the passageway, no one in the yard. Abruptly he pressed down on the circular disc, flung the door wide and lunged into the room, kicking the door closed with his heel behind him.

The woman screamed as Slater's hand shot out, seized Redshirt by the arm, jerked him upright.

"What the goddam hell you thi—"

Dow's rock hard fist smashed into the outlaw's jaw, knocked him sprawling back onto the bed and pinning the woman beneath him.

"Keep your mouth shut and you won't get hurt," Slater snarled at her as he reached for the outlaw's pants hanging from a bedpost.

"This a robbery?" she asked, squirming out from under Redshirt.

Slater's fingers were digging into the pockets of the garment. He touched a roll of bills, drew it out quickly, hurriedly thumbed through the currency . . . Five hundred dollars. There should be more if Reegan had split equally with his men. Again he went into Redshirt's pockets. Except for a few coins there was no more.

Taking possession of the currency, he threw the pants aside, and again casting a warning glance at the woman now sitting in the center of the bed viewing his actions with no interest, he turned the outlaw over, bound his wrists together and tied them to his feet, using strips made by ripping up one of the blankets.

Finishing off the job by gagging the man, Dow nodded to the woman.

"You're next. Stretch out there next to him."

"Go to hell, you goddam thief—"

Slater grabbed her by the neck, forced her into position beside Redshirt and bound her in like fashion. Stepping then to the door, he gave her a brief, hard smile.

"I'll be back," he said and moving through the door, closed and secured it with the hasp and pin.

21

Yellow light now filled the high-cut windows of the Great Western, and on beyond the saloon Slater could see that lamps had been lit elsewhere along the street, partly visible to him at the end of the passageway.

Taut, he stood motionless for several moments in the pale darkness, and then satisfied no one was coming, strode off along the row of cribs until he reached the one being occupied by Shorty and the woman in yellow. Stepping up to the door, he listened briefly, tried the latch. It had been fastened on the inside.

A gust of impatience ripped through him. Turning half about, he drew back, rammed his right shoulder into the flimsy panel. It flew inward under the impact, the crash of splintering wood mingling with the woman's startled scream.

Shorty leaped to his feet, lunged for the holstered gun lying atop his clothing on a nearby chair. Slater caught him with one hand, hit him with the other—a jolting blow to the jaw. The outlaw sagged, struggled to stay upright. Deadly methodic, Slater drew the man toward him, drove a second punishing fist to the chin. Shorty groaned, and, as Dow released him, staggered back against the wall and slowly settled to the floor.

Dow, breathing hard, cast a glance at the girl, a pale outline beyond the bed.

"Light a lamp," he ordered, pushing the shattered door into place. It had torn loose from its upper hinge and the board to which the latch was affixed had split from top to bottom.

He heard the woman strike a match, saw the flare of light, and then the lamp was aglow. "We'll have no trouble long as you keep quiet—and stay put," he said, reaching for Shorty's pants.

She nodded, fear showing on her features. She was a younger woman than the one with Redshirt, Slater noted as he pulled the fold of currency from the outlaw's pocket. He counted it quickly. Five hundred dollars. That amount was apparently all Reegan had given his men for their part in the robbery and murder—or he could be holding back a portion of a larger share to be paid later. Dow didn't think the outlaws had been in Goshen long enough to have spent any cash to speak of.

"Not robbing him," he explained to the girl, stuffing the money into his own pocket. "Just taking back what's mine. This man's an outlaw. He and the others he's with held me up. Killed three of my friends and took my money belt."

The woman frowned. "That other'n with Emma, did you—"

Slater nodded before she finished the question. "Left the both of them trussed up."

Jerking a cover off the bed he began to rip it into strips as he had done earlier, and, after gagging Shorty, tied him hand and foot and dragged him into a back corner of the room. Dow, an idea coming to him, turned then to the girl.

"What's your name?"

"They call me Goldie."

"All right, Goldie, I'll tell you how you can make fifty dollars real quick. I need some help getting the rest of that gang out here. Interested?"

The girl, finishing her dressing, came around the end of the bed and faced him. "What'll I have to do?"

"Bring the others out here to me—one at a time if you can manage it."

She frowned. "How? They seen Shorty going out with me. They'll be wondering—"

"Tell them Shorty's hurt, needs help."

Goldie shrugged. "All right, but what if they all come. There's four of them, one of you."

Slater gave that thought. Music was floating back from the saloon now, the steady plink of a piano, the sawing screech of a violin. Somewhere along the street a man shouted, drew an immediate response from farther on.

"Just have to handle it, somehow," Dow said. "Let me worry about that. Your job's to get them back here. There anybody in the next crib?"

"No, that's Cleo's. She's still inside."

"That's where I'll be . . . Let's get started. Don't want them blowing any more of that money than I can help."

Slater reached for the shattered door, opened it wide enough for their passage. Goldie did not move.

"Something bothering you?"

"Was just thinking—when this here's all over and you're gone, what'll happen to me? They'll know I tricked them and—"

"Nothing will happen to you. They'll all be in jail waiting to be hung for murder."

Goldie's shoulders stirred again in a gesture of acceptance, and, moving by him, turned into the yard. Slater, snatching up the torn blanket, followed, walked with her to the next hut. Entering, he listened to her fading footsteps while he made use of the time to further rip the bed cover into strips for later use.

There was no guarantee that he could depend on the girl, he realized; she could double-cross him, tip off Pete Reegan and the others as to what he was doing—it all depending upon how much fifty dollars meant to her. He smiled grimly in the darkness of the evil smelling little room; he had no choice but to take the risk. If she did turn against him, however, he'd be ready and . . .

He heard the thump of boot heels. Quickly crossing to the door, he peered out. Satisfaction rolled through him. Goldie had persuaded only one of the outlaws to accompany her. Pulling back into the blackness, Slater waited.

"What the hell's wrong with him?" a man's peevish voice demanded.

"How'd I know?" the girl shot back, equally irritated. "I ain't no doctor . . . Just sent me to get you. He's laying in there on the bed."

"Well, it sure better be something mighty important —hauling me out here like this," the man grumbled and pushed open the door.

Dow Slater's doubled fist came out of the darkness with all the force he could muster. The outlaw never knew what hit him, simply dropped slackly to the floor.

"Have any trouble?" he asked, removing the roll of currency from the unconscious man's pocket and thrusting it into his own. He'd count it later since time was short, but odds were there'd be no more or no less than the amounts possessed by Shorty and Redshirt. Grabbing several of the prepared strips of wool, Dow began to gag and tie the outlaw.

"No, just said Shorty'd sent me for him."

Slater, finished with his chore, picked up the man, hung him over his shoulder, nodded at the door. "Take a look; see if anybody's coming. Want to put him in with Shorty."

Goldie glanced into the yard. "Ain't nobody out there."

Dow moved by her, carried the outlaw to the adjacent hut and dumped him onto the bed. Shorty had not yet roused. Wheeling, he returned to where the girl was waiting.

"Going to need a different excuse this time—"

Goldie nodded slowly. "Ain't sure I can do it. Don't know what to say."

Reegan and the two other outlaws would be growing suspicious, Dow knew, but his only hope of recovering the money taken from him was to get them out of the Great Western and into a situation where he could deal with them on a purely physical basis.

"They still all together there at that table?"

"Yeh, just setting—drinking and talking. The boss, the

one they call Pete's telling about something he done down in Texas."

"Who's the one you just brought back?"

"Jubal—"

"You know the names of the others—besides Pete?"

"One's Fargo—he's kind of mean. Other'n's Dave something."

Slater rubbed at his skinned knuckles. "Can maybe handle Fargo and Dave, but Pete's something else. I know him; he'll go for his gun, then ask questions."

"Seemed kind of like the nicest one of the bunch."

Reegan would as soon kill you as draw a breath, Slater started to say and then checked his words. He didn't want to frighten the girl into backing out on him.

"Here's what you do," he said. "Go back in there, be sort of excited. Tell Fargo and Dave that Shorty and Jubal—and the one with your friend Emma—"

"Ike—"

"—and Ike are in trouble and want them to come give them a hand."

"What kind of trouble?"

"Say there's a big crap game going on with some cowpunchers and it looks like it's about to wind up in a scrap. That'll keep Pete Reegan out of it. He's not aiming to hurt his hands."

Goldie revolved his instructions over in her mind, turned and hurried toward the saloon. Pausing midway, she looked back. "You be waiting in the same shack?"

"Same one," Slater replied, and stepped back into the small room.

He would have to make it look real, and striking a match, he located a lamp, touched the small flame to its wick. Adjusting the light to a medium level, he glanced around. The trick would be to get the two outlaws into the room at the same moment—and that could be a problem.

He gave it thought, and then turning to the lone chair in the room, broke it into several pieces with his booted feet and placed them on the floor just inside the entrance. He crossed then to the lamp and pushed it to the back of the table, thus increasing the darkness of the doorway's threshold.

Satisfied, Slater stepped out onto the gravel landing and moving to the corner of the hut, took up a position there . . . The minutes dragged on. Goldie should be returning with the two outlaws if the scheme had worked. Uneasiness began to grow within him.

Had they gotten wise, realized that something was going on? Reegan was not a man easily fooled. Given some small inkling, he would catch on quick. Slater drew up suddenly. Four figures were emerging from the shadows alongside the saloon. He grinned bleakly. All three outlaws had responded to Goldie's summons . . . He'd bit off a big bite—now it was up to him to chew.

A moment later he breathed easier. The third person was not Reegan but another of the saloon women, one who had evidently taken up with Fargo or Dave. That lowered the odds a notch. Dow pulled back, crouched in the darkness, watched the two men now a step ahead of the women, approach.

They reached the front of the dimly lit shack, halted. One of the pair slowly drew his pistol, his movements barely discernible in the night.

"Shorty? Jube? Where the hell are you?"

"Inside," Goldie supplied.

The outlaw nearest to her turned. "Girlie, if this here's some kind of a trick, I'm going to beat the—"

"Take a look," the woman said, shrugging indifferently.

The other man moved cautiously toward the door. "Sure is quiet," he murmured. "Must be Jube and them's for sure got themselves into something bad . . . What say we rush them, Dave?"

Silently the second outlaw stepped to his partner's side. Both hunched, eased closer to the entrance. Little more than an arm's length away, Dow Slater tensed.

Abruptly Fargo and Dave lunged for the doorway. The latter, a half stride ahead, was the first to encounter the pile of chair fragments. His feet shot out from under him. He rocked back, collided solidly with Fargo. Both men staggered to one side. In that same instant Slater drove into them, hurling himself through the entry and crashing full force into the stumbling pair.

His charge sent Fargo head-on into a wall with a sickening thud. Dave, more fortunate, reeled into the bed, tripped and went over its end, clawing out his gun. The weapon went off with a blinding flash, filling the shack with a deafening blast and swirling powder smoke. Slater, feeling the heat of the bullet along his neck as he threw himself on the outlaw, struck out with both fists at the man's face. He felt the flesh give beneath his hammering but only when Dave went limp did he pull back.

Breathing hard, he drew himself upright. He could hear voices up near the saloon, knew the gunshot had been noticed and would likely bring the curious seeking its source. He wheeled to the doorway. Goldie was in the yard immediately opposite. She was alone, the other woman apparently having taken flight. Slater made a gesture toward the Great Western.

"Head them off . . . Tell them the shot came from down the way."

He didn't wait to see if she understood or complied, but swung back into the reeking room. Moving fast he dug the roll of bills from Dave's pocket, hastily tied the man securely and rolled him into a far corner. Turning then, he relieved Fargo of his share of the cash and used the last of the blanket strips to bind him.

It had all been quickly done, and still sucking for breath, Slater stepped to the door, glanced around. There was no sign of Goldie, and looking toward the rear of the saloon, he saw that whatever crowd had begun to gather there was gone. The woman had succeeded in diverting the curious.

Moving out onto the landing, he leaned back against the wall of the shack, grateful for a few moments' rest. Only Pete Reegan remained, and getting him to . . .

"Stand easy, mister," a voice said coldly from the darkness at the corner of the hut. "Else I'll blow your head off."

22

Slater stiffened. It was Reegan. The gunshot and the failure of his friends to return had brought him out to see
what was taking place. In the dark he had circled the
cribs, come in from their rear. Dow swore silently. He'd
been careless—and it was going to cost him his life, most
likely.

"Reach—slow and easy—"

Slater raised his arms. He could hear the crunch of
gravel as the outlaw moved up behind him.

"What the hell's this all about? Where's Jube and Fargo
—all the others?"

Reegan waited for no reply, but stepped warily around
Dow, threw a quick glance into the hut. He caught a
glimpse of Fargo and Dave.

"All right—get inside, goddam you!" he snarled. "I aim
to find out what's going on."

Pete Reegan had so far failed to recognize him, Slater
realized, backing into the doorway. He slid a look toward the saloon hopeful of a returning crowd. The yard
was deserted, lay dark and silent.

Inside the shack he pushed back against a wall, shoulders flat to the rough-surfaced boards. Cautious, Reegan,
the muzzle of his pistol never straying from its line on

Slater's chest, moved past him. Reaching the lamp he turned up the wick. Light flooded the room. Flicking the motionless figures on the floor with his eyes, he came about. The outlaw's jaw sagged.

"Slater! Left you laying dead back in that wash—"

"Not quite," Dow said coldly, anger beginning to throb within him.

The outlaw was regarding him intently. "Wondered what'd happened to you after that little ruckus in Powderville . . . Was somebody in Dodge saying you'd hung up your guns. Told him I didn't believe it."

Slater made no comment, his gaze locked to that of Reegan.

"Seen I was wrong back there at the wash. You sure wasn't packing iron . . . Mite hard staying alive after what you've been through, ain't it?"

"Been getting by."

Reegan grinned. "No more, you ain't! Owe you for that little deal in Powderville. Cost me some good boys —boys that'd been with me quite a spell and knew the ropes—"

"Some other folks died there, too—people that had nothing to do with it."

"You mean that sodbuster and his woman? Hell, they just run out of luck."

"No, you used them, Pete, waited until they got in front of you knowing they'd be dead if trouble started."

"Was a kind of a cute trick," the outlaw said, looking closely at Dow. He had been drinking heavily but it was noticeable only in his eyes and a slight deliberateness in his movements. "That why you shucked your gun and quit lawing?"

Pete Reegan was toying with him, Slater knew, dragging out the moments with useless conversation, reveling in the fear and desperation he hoped to excite . . . It could work both ways. If he could keep the outlaw talking, cause him to relax his guard for only a brief moment, the opportunity to overpower the man might present itself.

"Was part of it," he said.

"Kind of hard to swallow that," Reegan said with a slow shake of his head. "You been wearing a badge a long time. Can't see you going soft when you see somebody get plugged."

That wasn't it, Slater was finally realizing; it was the constancy of death, the relentless accumulation of lifeless bodies for which he was either responsible or had borne witness over the years; Powderville was just the breaking point. But it was useless to explain it to the outlaw. He would never understand.

Slater glanced through the open doorway into the yard. He thought he had heard a sound, but he saw no one, reckoned it had come from the street.

"Mind if I put down my arms? Getting tired—"

"Keep them up," Reegan cut in. "Not taking any chances with you . . . Where's Shorty and the rest of my boys?"

"Tied up in a couple of the cribs . . . Like to know something."

"Yeh?"

"How'd you know I'd be carrying cash money instead of a bank draft when I left McCoy? Somebody told you about that same as they probably told you about the drive."

Reegan's mouth pulled into a hard grin. "Yeh, somebody sure did. And I reckon where you're going soon's I get my boys together, it won't hurt none for you to know."

"You want to pay me my fifty dollars now?"

Goldie's voice came from the landing. Seeing Dow Slater only through the doorway, she believed him alone.

Pete Reegan's attention wavered for the merest fraction of time. Slater, desperate, knowing his minutes were numbered, reacted instantly. He kicked out. The toe of his boot struck the barrel of the pistol in the outlaw's hand just as Reegan, disconcerted briefly by the saloon girl's unexpected appearance, jerked back around.

The weapon discharged in a surge of sound and smoke. Slater felt the searing shock of a bullet driving into his leg. He seized the outlaw's pistol in one hand, locked the fingers of the other about Reegan's throat.

Together they reeled about the room, each striving to break clear of the other. Dow felt his legs come up against the bed. He tripped, went off balance. Immediately Pete Reegan pulled back, kneed him viciously in the groin.

Gasping from pain, Slater clung to the weapon and again they began to wrestle back and forth, colliding with one wall, rebounding into another, crashing into the table, the end of the bed. Slater's head was pounding with pain and he could feel his leg weakening under him, but he hung on, knowing that if he lost his grip on the pistol he was a dead man.

They rocked again into the table. The lamp tipped, all but fell to the floor. Heaving, grunting, sweat slicking their skin, blinding their eyes, they reeled toward the door. Slater tried to spin, throw the outlaw off balance. The effort failed but Reegan did stumble into the remnants of the shattered chair laid for Fargo and Dave.

For an instant his hold on the weapon slackened, Dow, throwing all his reserve strength into it, jerked it free— but only for a breath. The outlaw grabbed it with both hands, wrenched hard. Abruptly it went off. Slater felt the flame scorch the skin of his chest through the fabric of his shirt and his ears closed suddenly from the effects of the nearby blast.

And in the next moment Pete Reegan was falling away from him, a wondering frown on his dark features as if he could not understand what had happened.

Slater stepped back, allowed the outlaw to settle slowly on the floor, back against the side of the bed. The pistol dangled loosely in the man's stiffening fingers and a dull glaze was overtaking his eyes.

Gasping for breath, pain hammering relentlessly at him, Slater reached down, opened Reegan's shirt, rapidly staining from a gaping wound in the chest. The money belt he'd bought from Tallman was around the man's waist. Blood was trickling down onto it, and fighting the hollowness that was spreading through him, Dow released the buckle and pulled the strap free. He peered closely at the outlaw.

"Pete—who was it that tipped you off?"

Reegan's sagging lids lifted slightly. "What?"

"Who told you about the drive—the money?"

The outlaw's lips curled downward. A tremor shook him. "Go to hell," he mumbled, and toppled sideways.

A small crowd had gathered outside the doorway to the hut. Slater became aware of that as he drew himself upright. His leg was now throbbing dully, keeping pace with the pain in his head, and ignoring both he laid out the money belt on the bed. Sinking onto the corn-shuck mattress, he began to open the pockets.

"Man there's Pete Reegan," he said to the faces staring at him from the doorway. "Wanted in Kansas—a half a dozen other places for murder and robbery. This money belongs to me."

As a quick buzz of comment broke out, Slater carefully counted the cash removed from the belt . . . An even three thousand dollars. He had recovered twenty-five hundred, more or less, from the remaining outlaws, making a round figure total of fifty-five hundred in their possession. There was still twenty-five hundred dollars missing.

Slater's jaw hardened. It could be but one place, in the pockets of the man who had kept Reegan posted—a man the outlaw had refused to name but whose identity had become more firmly established in Slater's mind with each passing hour . . . No sweat . . . He'd collect the rest of Glenna Darrow's money for her once he was back in Shibolem.

Stuffing the bills and gold pieces back into the belt, Dow hung it over his shoulder and got stiffly to his feet. Bending down, he picked up Reegan's flat-crowned hat, the trade-mark by which the outlaw had come to be known. He stared at it briefly and then, turning, placed it over the man's slack face, and moved on to the doorway.

In the forefront of the crowd Goldie looked up at him expectantly. He gave her a tight smile, said, "I'll square things with you in a minute," and put his attention on the men behind her.

"Can prove everything I've told you if need be," he said in a dragging voice as he leaned against the door frame. "Right now I'm needing help. Got four men that I want locked up in your jail. There's another the doctor best look at—he could be dead. Call your undertaker for Reegan, there."

"Looks like you could use the doc yourself," a voice called from the crowd.

Dow Slater nodded wryly. "Reckon so, and soon as some of you get done what I've asked, I'll look him up. Don't want any of that bunch to get away."

"They won't." It was Wingate, the saddler. He was pushing through the tightly packed group, motioning to several of the bystanders to follow. "Where you got the rest of them?"

"Crib next door—and the second one from the end. You'll find a lady in that one. Don't bother her. She just got caught in the squeeze."

Wingate bobbed. "Be some papers for you to sign. I've

helped the marshal with things like this before. Where'll you be?"

"At my place," Goldie said, stepping up and taking Slater by the arm. "And you send Doc over there first, hear? That outlaw bum can wait."

23

Tip Weber was the key. Slater had become convinced of that when, on the tenth day following the recovery of Glenna Darrow's money from Reegan and his men, he rode into Shibolem.

Still a bit stiff and sore from his wounds, Dow had ridden out of Goshen at the first opportunity, anxious to make the return. Like as not the Darrows had given him up long ago, having come to the conclusion that either outlaws had attacked him and the crew, robbing him and killing all, or that he had simply skipped with the money after ridding himself of the three Circle D cowhands. A hard smile twisted Slater's lips; which version would Ed Gault be endorsing?

The deputy was in for a surprise. That he was behind the scheme and in league with Pete Reegan, seemed certain. His actions during and after the drive was over all pointed to it—and he had wanted Glenna Darrow to fail. Whether he had intended originally to profit so handsomely from it was yet to be answered, but if it was true then it was logical to assume that he still had his share of the money.

But proof was needed before he could be sure of the deputy's guilt, and that could come from Tip Weber, the

man who had come to camp that night purposely to draw
him into a shootout. Failing in that, Weber, with his two
friends aiding, had endeavored to force a fight in which
the end would find him badly beaten and unable to continue with the cattle drive.

That, too, had backfired on them and their visit had
wound up with them being securely tied prisoners who
mysteriously managed an escape shortly after Ed Gault
had put in an appearance.

Too, Ed Gault was one of only four persons besides
himself who knew he would be paid off in cash for the
herd, and the others—Tallman, Royce Darrow, and Lewis,
the cattle buyer—could hardly be considered suspects.
Dow had given thought to the possibility of the storekeeper being involved, had ruled it out. Tallman was
known as an honest man, had been in business for
years and was well-to-do in his own right. He'd not risk
all for so paltry a share.

Halting at the end of the street, he sat for a time with
his glance on the window of the Home Cafe. Judith would
be inside, busy at making ready for the noon trade. Off
and on during the past days she had come into his mind,
stirring up pleasant memories, and he wondered now
what she thought of him. Would she believe, as most others undoubtedly did, that he had stolen the Darrows'
money? Or would she have enough faith in him to reject
the belief? He realized suddenly that knowing the answer was important to him, but it would have to wait;
finding Tip Weber must come before all else.

Swinging left, he rode up to the rear of the Calico Girl

saloon, Tip's favored hangout. There were no horses at the hitchrack, but Dow dismounted, had his look through the dusty side window of the building, anyway. He saw only three patrons in the place, none of them Weber.

Moving back to the horse he'd purchased in Goshen, a fairly good little buckskin, he swung onto the saddle, and still hoping to avoid being noticed, circled to the alley and rode quickly to Happy Jack's. There was no sign of Weber there, either, the saloon in fact only barely open with the swamper doing his cleaning chores and a woman behind the bar washing glasses in preparation for business to come.

At a loss, Slater again mounted, brushed at the sweat on his face. He was undecided where best to look next for the rider, and he was reluctant to continue on for the Circle D without satisfying the several questions that were unanswered. In the next moment he saw two men come from the rear of the Prairie Rose and turn toward the stable. Satisfaction rolled through Slater. It was Weber. Roweling the buckskin, he sent the horse loping for the hotel.

Tip heard him coming, wheeled lazily. Surprise blanked his dark features. His hand dropped to the pistol on his hip. Slater shook his head and raised both hands to show he was unarmed.

"Want to talk," he said, drawing the buckskin to a halt, and climbing down.

Weber, eyes narrowed, considered him sullenly. "We ain't got nothing to talk about—"

The man with him was Pike, one of the two who had

been along that night on the drive. Face stolid, he stepped slowly to one side. Dow jerked a thumb at him.

"Tell your friend to stay put. I've got no quarrel with him—with you either. Just looking for the answer to a couple of questions."

Tip relaxed slightly, shrugged. "Everybody round here figured you'd blowed the country—or was dead."

"Just took longer getting back than I figured."

Weber threw a glance back up the alley. "If you're just coming in where's Tom Farley and the others?"

Slater watched the man closely. "Dead—murdered, and if you don't want to find yourself mixed up in their killings, you'll talk up."

Tip Weber drew up sharply. "Now, wait just a damned minute! Don't go trying to frame me, mister! I don't know nothing about no killings!"

"Maybe—but you know about this sure'n hell—did Ed Gault hire you to come to my camp that night and try to rimram me into a fight?"

Weber shook his head. "I ain't saying nothing," he replied with a side look at Pike.

"Up to you, but if you're scared to talk then I'll take it that you had a hand in the robbery and killings. The U. S. Marshal will figure it that way, too."

"Don't go dragging me in on something like that!" Pike said, his voice rising. "All I know is—"

"Sure it was Ed," Weber interrupted. "Wasn't no big deal. Said he didn't want you getting that herd through."

"Why?"

"Well, he didn't do much talking about it but he was

fearing the Darrow gal'd back out on marrying him if she got her hands on a lot of money and could start making something out of the ranch again . . . And something else, he figured she was getting kind of sweet on you."

"And he hired you to put a bullet in me—"

"Yeh, was just going to wing you, lay you up enough so's you couldn't make the drive. He said she'd call it off then because Tom Farley and them other two old codgers sure couldn't handle it."

Slater rubbed at his whiskered jaw. It was hard to believe that Ed Gault would go to such lengths, but there was no doubt that he had, and this strengthened his suspicions.

"Did Gault set it up with an outlaw named Reegan to raid the herd when he wasn't able to stop the drive?"

Tip Weber frowned, wagged his head. "I don't know nothing about no outlaw. He just hired me to fix you good . . . Somebody try to rustle the herd?"

"They tried," Slater answered, wheeling to his horse and going onto the saddle. A fleeting expression of pain crossed his face as he settled on the hull. The wound in his leg still bothered him at times and he knew he should have given it more time to heal, as the doctor in Goshen had suggested. But he felt it was important that he return to Shibolem as soon as possible.

"You know if Gault's around?"

"Sure, he's around, but not much," Weber said, grinning. "Spending most of his time at the Darrows. They're getting things all set for the marrying—like he's been wanting. Prob'ly find him out there."

"Obliged," Slater said and cutting the buckskin about, doubled back to the street.

He had been right about the deputy. Gault had tried to prevent the sale of the Darrows' cattle for his own selfish purposes. It stood to reason that failing in a first attempt, he would make a second—one that involved Pete Reegan and his gang.

Undoubtedly he did not anticipate any killing in the process and would have had no wish for this to occur. But at such times things did get out of hand, and that was how Ed Gault would look at it; it was bad luck, certainly not something he had wanted.

Deep in thought as he moved out for the Darrow ranch, Slater suddenly became conscious that he was riding down the center of Shibolem's main street, that persons along the walks were pausing to stare at him in wonder.

He swung his attention to the Home Cafe. Judith, eyes wide, her lips parted in surprise, was standing in the doorway. Raising a hand he touched the brim of his hat with a forefinger, smiled. It would please her to learn that he hadn't gone back to the old ways—that he still was carrying no gun.

24

They had gathered in the small enclosed porch at the rear of the ranch house, were sitting around the table drinking coffee when Dow Slater rode in and halted at the hitchrack.

Through the vines he could see Mrs. Darrow, Royce, Deputy Sheriff Ed Gault, and Glenna. The girl looked to be far from her usual confident self, was now subdued, almost morose. Her plans of rebuilding the Circle D and becoming a successful rancher in her own right had died when it became apparent the cash for the herd, upon which she was banking so heavily, was lost, leaving her to face a future she evidently did not relish as the wife of a lawman.

Removing the money belt from around his waist, Slater circled the corner of the house and crossed to the door. Grim set, he drew it open, stepped inside.

For a long, breathless moment the four at the table stared, astonishment draining their features. And then Glenna cried out, leaped to her feet. Running to Dow she threw her arms about him.

"I knew you weren't dead—that you'd come back!"

Slater gently disengaged himself, eyes never leaving Ed Gault, now upright and watching him closely. He wondered how the deputy had explained his absence to the girl at the time the outlaws attacked, wondered, too, if Darrow, regarding him now as always with narrow contempt, had owned up to his irresponsibility.

Stepping back from Glenna who seemed unwilling or unable to move, he tossed the money belt onto the table.

"It's twenty-five hundred dollars short," he said. "Along with a short hundred I had to use for expenses."

The girl turned to the strap at once, began to open the pockets. "Twenty-five hundred dollars," she repeated slowly. "What—where is it?"

Slater leaned back against the wall, gave his accounting of the drive and what had taken place afterward. Mrs. Darrow began to weep when he related the deaths of the three cowhands, and Gault, surprise finally overcome, nodded briskly.

"Glad you run down that bunch—"

Dow studied him coolly. "Yeh, expect you are."

"Then you think whoever it was that tipped off this Reegan has the rest of the money?"

"Only place it could be—and it's somebody who knew I was getting paid off in cash."

"Was a half a dozen jaspers hanging around Tallman's when I was there," Royce Darrow said. "Any one of them could've seen that cattle buyer paying you off."

"Nobody saw it, was careful about that. And the only ones knowing I got cash were you, the buyer, Tallman, and the deputy, here," Slater said fixing his attention on Gault. "Nobody else."

The deputy's head came back. His face slowly flushed. "You trying to say it was me?" he demanded angrily.

A silence filled the porch. Glenna, frowning, turned to Gault. Mrs. Darrow continued to sob quietly. Royce drew a cigar from his shirt pocket, thrust it between his teeth.

"By God—nobody calls me a thief!" the deputy shouted.

"Then maybe you'd best explain why you hired Tip Weber and a couple others to jump me, try to bung me up so's I couldn't make the drive. And when that didn't work you got word to Pete Reegan—"

"That ain't so!" Gault declared, and then hesitating, he lowered his head. "Reckon I did put Tip to doing what you said, but that's all."

Glenna stared at him, aghast. "Why? In Heaven's name —why?"

"Wanted you to forget this ranching thing, marry me like we'd planned . . . And then you was kind of shining up to him and I figured if he got the herd through and brought back all that money, I could just forget what we were aiming to do."

"Were you the one who tipped off the outlaws?" Glenna's voice was level, firm. "Have you got the rest of my money?"

"No! I'll swear to that on a stack of Bibles!" Gault replied hurriedly. Sweat lay in patches on his face and his mouth worked convulsively. "With God as my witness, Glenna—it wasn't me!"

The girl studied the deputy in cold silence. Finally she

turned to Slater. "I believe him. It was somebody else, somebody there in McCoy most likely."

Dow shrugged wearily. There was now no doubt in his mind either that it had not been Gault. That the lawman was partly guilty was true—he had admitted to such—but it ended there. The answer to who had been responsible for the ambush, the deaths of Kargill, John Ledge, and Farley, and the theft of the money, lay, as Glenna had suggested, back at the railhead . . . Maybe his ruling out the storekeeper, Tallman, had been a mistake. He'd start with him.

"I'll be heading back to McCoy," he said heavily. "Feel it's up to me to get that money back for you."

Gault nodded, relief in his eyes. "Take it as a favor if you'll let me ride with you. Mighty important to me that we catch whoever it is," he said, shifting his glance to the girl.

Glenna looked away, ignoring him. "It's a lot of money," she murmured. "We need it—badly."

Royce Darrow stirred. "Far as I can see you'll be wasting your time," he said. Reaching down, he picked up his hat, set it on his head at a jaunty angle. "Hell, Glenna, you've got plenty there—forget the rest . . . I'm going in to town. Ed, you coming?"

Slater came to attention, a deep frown puckering his brow. The band encircling the crown of Darrow's hat was of woven horsehair, studded with brass buttons. Only once before in his life had he seen one like it—that day in the Powderville bank on the plainsman style hat being worn by Pete Reegan.

In the next moment anger gripped Dow Slater. Goshen . . . That night in the shack . . . Reegan lying dead on the floor . . . He had picked up the outlaw's hat, placed it over the man's face, vaguely aware that there was something different. It came to him now. The fancy strip of horsehair and brass he'd noticed in Powderville had been missing.

"That hat band," he said in a quiet voice, "where'd you get it?"

Royce started, eyes narrowing once again, and then he made a gesture of dismissal with his hand. "Oh, bought it from a jasper I run into."

"Who? What was his name?"

Glenna looked up at Dow, puzzled. "What difference does it make?"

"Plenty. That band belonged to Pete Reegan," Slater said. "Means Royce has been hanging around him."

There was a long breath of stunned silence, and then Glenna whirled to her brother. "I might have known you'd have something to do with it!" she cried. "You never were any account—never will be! What did you do with the money?"

Darrow pushed back from the table. There was a whiteness around his mouth. "You taking that drifter's word for this?"

"I am—and I know he's right!" the girl said. "You've been spending a lot lately—new boots, a gold watch and a ring—where'd you get the cash for them?"

"Seen you at the Calico Girl doing a lot of gambling, too," the deputy added, his features stern.

Royce stood motionless. A wildness filled his eyes. He glanced from one to the other seemingly undecided what next to do—seek safety in flight or give in. He looked down at his mother. Abruptly his shoulders lowered. Shrugging, he nodded.

"Yeh, was me, all right . . . Money, what's left of it's in my room in that old tin box Pa used to keep his cash in."

Mrs. Darrow was now stonily silent, her gaze fixed on her son. Glenna, the truth suddenly indisputable, stared at him in shock and disbelief.

"Royce! How could you do that to me—and Mama?"

Darrow's mouth tightened. "Was tired of playing second fiddle to you, that's how. I'm the man of this house, but it was always you taking charge."

"Only because you were never sober long enough to do anything—"

"Maybe I'd of had a reason to, if you'd given me the chance," Royce snapped. "Anyway, you're getting most of your damned money back. No use carrying on like you are. You either, Ma."

Glenna sighed, turned away from him. Mrs. Darrow murmured, "Poor Aaron and Tom and Johnny Ledge," in a lost sort of voice.

"Yeh, was you that got them killed," Gault said, pointing a finger at Royce. "Going to have to do some talking about that."

Dow Slater backed slowly toward the door. The matter was settled as far as he was concerned. What remained lay between the family, and the law. He nodded to the girl.

"Can find me in town if you—"

"Don't leave," she cut in, following him into the yard. "You've got your pay coming—and I want you to stay on, take the job I offered."

He shook his head. "Obliged to you, but no."

"It could mean a lot more than just a job, Dow—a life together for us—a good life."

He stood for a moment looking off across the hardpack, then: "No, I'm not the man for you. Saw again what wearing a gun leads to and I'm more set than ever against one . . . Man you need can't feel the way I do."

"You'll get over that in time," Glenna said soberly. "It just has to wear off."

Slater was silent for a long breath. "I don't want it to," he said at last, and giving her a tight smile, turned toward his horse. "So long."

He did not listen for her reply, but mounted, wheeled about and, roweling the buckskin, set out for town at a brisk lope . . . Judith would be waiting for him.